The Riddle of the
Frozen Phantom

Other titles by Margaret Mahy

The Riddle of the Frozen Phantom

Margaret Mahy
Illustrated by Chris Mould

An imprint of HarperCollinsPublishers

A Vanessa Hamilton book

First published by Collins 2001
Collins is an imprint of HarperCollinsPublishers Ltd
77-85 Fulham Palace Road, Hammersmith,
London, W6 8JB

The HarperCollins website address is:
www.fireandwater.com

3 5 7 9 8 6 4 2

Text copyright © Margaret Mahy 2001

ISBN 0 00 711374 9

Margaret Mahy asserts the moral right to be identified as the author of the work.

Printed and bound in Great Britain by
Omnia Books Limited, Glasgow

Contents

CHAPTER 1

At the Very Back of the Drawer

Suddenly, something *clonked* softly at the back of the empty drawer.

Sophie Sapwood, sitting in a sea of old photographs, stopped listening to her brothers who were outside, shouting and whistling as they bounced on the family trampoline. She tuned in to the back of the drawer instead.

She had been planning to go out to the trampoline herself, just to show both brothers the best way to turn somersaults in the air. After all, she had already found what she had been searching for — photographs of their dead mother which she had studied carefully. There was nothing left to look for. The drawer was completely empty.

But it wasn't! It couldn't be! Somewhere at the very back of the drawer, somewhere behind that first empty openness, something had clonked softly. Sophie tugged at the drawer, trying to pull it right out, but it remained obstinately jammed halfway. Reaching in once more, her searching fingers spidered left, then spidered right. Nothing! But then, by flattening her arm, Sophie managed to reach just a little further and her fingertips brushed something smooth. Whatever it was was also icy cold, which was unexpected on such a warm morning. After all, here in New Zealand it was nearly midsummer — nearly Christmas.

The night before, Sophie had dreamed about her mother. She had woken and lain in bed for a few minutes without actually opening her eyes while she tried to work out if her mother had really looked like the mother in the dream. It had bothered Sophie to find that, though she could remember her mother's voice, though she could remember the songs she had sung and her way of laughing, she was no longer sure about the colour of her hair, or the shape of her nose. That was why she had sneaked upstairs, all on her own, to sort through the bottom drawer in an old forgotten chest of drawers, boxed in by family junk at the back of the upstairs spare room. This drawer was crammed with photographs — some of Sophie's mother, some of her big brother, Edward, and her little brother, Hotspur, and some of Sophie herself. Most of the photographs, however, showed icebergs, distant mountains and her father, the famous Antarctic explorer, Bonniface Sapwood, proudly posing beside sledges, flags and whole parties of penguins. There were even one or two photographs of the redheaded penguin-expert Corona Wottley, who had been part of an exploring expedition Bonniface had organised several years ago.

Sophie had patiently worked her way right through that jam-packed, higgelty-piggelty, mish-mash of Antarctic photographs until she had entirely emptied the drawer... or at least, she thought she had. Yet here she was, touching this clicking, cold shape; this whatever-it-was which must have been left and lost for years and years. Scrabbling busily, she got a grip on it. Gently, she drew it out into the light of day.

Dangling from her dusty fingers was a yellowish-white pendant – a milky tear carved from a bone. Whalebone, perhaps, thought Sophie. It was threaded on a thin strip of leather rather like a long bootlace. The greenish light, filtering through the ivy that half-covered the upstairs window, seemed to love this pendant, stroking it, then sinking into it. Sophie loved it too – loved it so much that she immediately hung it around her neck and then, leaping across the room, stared at herself in the dusty mirror above the old dressing table.

How strange! The pendant had changed her. She had suddenly become a girl with a secret. She touched it wonderingly. It must have been shut up in the drawer for years and years, and during that time no one had worn it or warmed it or wanted it. It's *meant* for me, thought Sophie. Even though Christmas was a whole five days away she felt that the house had given her a sort of early Christmas present. "It's meant for me," she repeated aloud, and nobody argued or contradicted her. However, just to be on the safe side, she slipped the pendant down under her T-shirt. For some reason she felt certain that, although it wanted to be worn, it also wanted to be hidden. Perhaps there was something it needed to hide from.

As it slid down over her heart, stroking her warm skin, Sophie gasped, for it still felt as cold as – no!

even *colder* than ice! She clapped both hands against her chest as if she were in pain. But within a second or two the pendant began to feel a little less cold. Sophie's skin was working on it.

Aha! I'm the boss! thought Sophie, and began packing photographs back into the drawer, but neatly this time. She looked at the photographs of her mother all over again.

We *do* look alike, she thought. That means she's still here in a way. I'm watching the world for both of us. And this thought made her happy.

She leaped up, made for the door and pounded down the stairs on her way out to play with her brothers on the family trampoline.

There was no way that Sophie could have known as she hopped from one step to another, with the pendant slowly warming up against her skin, that far away, in a lost part of the wild Antarctic coast, a pair of eyes that had been closed for a long, long time were opening. Someone – someone who had not moved for the last seventy years – had begun to stir.

CHAPTER 2

A Strange Awakening

"Cold!" that someone muttered, hugging himself. "I'm so cold!"

Although he was in a cold place, it wasn't the cold around him he was feeling. The cold about which he was complaining seemed to be welling out of his very heart. At first that was the only thing he really knew. He certainly wasn't sure who he was or even *what* he was (though a lot of people feel like this when they wake from deep sleep). He struggled to open his eyes properly and, at long last, he *did* open them, looking out into a deep and ancient darkness stained with strange blue light. When he turned his head, this light turned too, as if it were somehow *watching* him. And horrakapotchkin! What was that directly above him? Long teeth, preparing to bite him in two? The fangs of a ferocious beast?

Frozen with cold! Frozen with terror! the waking man thought. But is the world freezing me or am I freezing the world?

But the faint blue light seemed to be soaking into those teeth. Of course! They were not *really* teeth. They were icicles. The man took a deep breath.

"Who am I?" he asked aloud. "Where am I? What am I doing here? And why?" He shook some of these questions out of his spinning head. "Pull yourself together!" he told himself sternly. "One thing at a time! Now! Who am I? I am… I am…"

"The Captain!" said a voice in his head – his own voice. "You are the Captain!"

"Right!" he said aloud. "I remember now! I am the Captain! Well, if I'm the Captain I should be up and doing, not lying around in the dark." And, flattening himself, he began sliding out from under those glassy teeth. To his amazement, he felt, as he wriggled and slid, that he was much lighter than he had somehow imagined he would be. Indeed, it was as if he weighed nothing at all. This unexpected lightness unbalanced him. He wobbled! He swung one arm into the air. Immediately, the longest tooth of ice plunged greedily into it. The Captain screwed up his eyes, expecting blood and pain, but there was no blood, and no pain either. He lowered his arm and the glassy tooth slid out of it without leaving a single mark even on the sleeve of his heavy jacket. Flattening himself once more, he wriggled out from under the toothy icicles, swung his legs sideways, stood up carefully and looked out into the darkness.

The strange blue glow was slowly eating into the shadows around him. It seemed to be coming from him, seeping out of the folds and wrinkles of his clothes. And suddenly the Captain knew exactly where he was. He had been lying on his very own bunk, in his very own cabin, on his very own ship – the gallant *Riddle*.

His fingers, muffled in three pairs of fine woollen gloves, crept across the fur collar of his great jacket. Horrakapotchkin! His ears had disappeared. But then he realised he was wearing his balaclava and two knitted hats, and that his ears were tucked quite safely beneath them. He fingered the high collar of his natural wool jersey and below that his shirt, the top of his long johns and then not just one but three layers of underwear. He was searching for his whalebone good-luck charm – a charm he had carved and polished himself during his very first Antarctic winter night, back before he rose to the rank of captain. He had shared many adventures with that charm and believed it had carried him safely through many dangers.

"Where's my pendant?" he asked aloud. The sound of his own echoing voice frightened him. "Hang on! You're going too fast!" he told himself in a stern whisper. "Begin again! Now, I'm the captain. Right! I'm in my cabin. Right! There's my captain's desk! What's that lumpy thing sitting on it? Oh, it must be the ship's logbook. But what's happened to it? Oh, I see! It's covered with ice. And it's very thick ice. I must have been asleep for ages." He puzzled for a moment, then shrugged and went on. "Never mind! What really matters is that my memory is rushing back safe and sound from wherever it has been."

But this was where the Captain's memory stopped rushing back. He found he had absolutely no idea of where in the Antarctic *The Riddle* might happen to be. "Look around!" he told himself sternly. "Work it out!"

So he peered this way and that into the gloom, noticing there was ice underfoot and ice overhead, and at last he stood up and made for the cabin door which he tried to open. The blueish light moved with him.

But the door was iced shut. Why, he could not even turn the door handle! The Captain pushed hard. Nothing moved. He put his shoulder to the door and tried to jolt it open with good old-fashioned sailor-power.

Almost at once, he found himself standing on the other side of the door, looking back at it in surprise. Had it opened? No! Somehow, he seemed to have gone straight through it, ice and all. Odd! Very odd! He thumped it experimentally. *Bang!* It seemed quite solid. He thumped harder and this time his hand sank deep into the ice and wood. The Captain pulled his hand free and frowned down at his faintly glowing, gloved fingers.

He shrugged. "Perhaps all doors are like that," he murmured (though deep down he knew they weren't). "I might have forgotten," (though deep down he knew he hadn't). "I've been fast asleep, and now it's taking me a minute or two to remember the way things ought to be."

Ahead he saw faint, blueish light coming down

the companionway. Where were his officers? Where was his crew? Above all, where was his old friend, the First Mate, Escher Black? There wasn't even the smallest cabin boy in sight. "All hands aft!" he shouted, just in case, but no one joined in with a cheery, "Aye aye, Sir!" He tried again. "Escher! Escher Black! Heave to, Escher!"

Silence!

"I've lost my pendant and I've lost my memory. I've lost my ship's crew and I've lost my best friend," he said to himself, climbing the companionway. "Something terrible must have happened for Escher Black would never desert me. But I mustn't waste time worrying. I must *remember*! Now! Why does *The Riddle* look so strange? I do know ships don't usually look like this. It really is a riddle."

For the ship seemed hung about with frozen sails and veils of ice. Ice curved all the way around *The Riddle*. Ice arched over it, masts and all. I'm in a cave, thought the Captain (looking high, looking low as he worked things out). So he was.

The cave was dim, but not quite dark. Light, rather like the light that was still seeping out of the Captain himself, was finding its way through cracks and twisting shafts in the white, glittering roof. It was beautiful but very puzzling.

A slanting bridge, swollen with ice, connected the icy ship to the frozen land. That must be the gangplank, thought the Captain. I'll just slither down it, walk off a little way and look back at The Riddle. If I put a bit of distance between me and the ship — if I look back at it — I might get some clues.

But he couldn't walk down that gangplank. It wasn't just the iciness of it. He couldn't so much as set foot on it. Whenever he tried, the air seemed to thicken and freeze in front of him. Try as he might, he could not take a single step away from The Riddle.

Suddenly, the Captain understood! He wasn't an ordinary captain any more. He was a ghost captain... a phantom... a spook! He wasn't living on The Riddle (wherever it might happen to be), he was haunting it. He must be dead.

Just for a moment the Captain was terrified.

"Help!" he cried aloud. His ghost voice sprang away from him like a salt sea breeze. It swirled around the cave then shot off towards the bright, outside world. "Help! Help! Help!" the Captain cried three times. "Help! Help! Help!" went the echoes, on and on, up into the overhead tunnels through which the light was seeping into the cave, and out into the unknown space beyond.

The captain heard his own echoes fly outwards

and upwards, but there was no reply. He was all alone, haunting a lost ship, in an unknown cave, somewhere in a desert of ice. He would have wept with despair if he hadn't been the ghost of a particularly brave man.

What he did not know was that his three cries for help were already flying at great speed through the outside world, every one of them determined to find the right listener.

CHAPTER 3

The First Listener

"Help!" went the Captain's first call.

If an ordinary person had shouted "Help!" the cry would have dissolved into the Antarctic air. But the Captain had called out in a ghost voice. His first cry flew like a stormy petrel across the islands and salt seas of the great Southern Ocean. It flew above schools of whales and crossed the secret airy routes of the wandering albatross until it came to New Zealand, a country made up of islands, jam-packed with possible listeners.

Most ears are closed to a ghost cry. All the same, some ghost cries can be very persistent. This one searched for a special ear – an ear that would welcome it and invite it in, and at last it found one. It curled its way through the caves and tunnels of this ear, and into the sleeper's dreams.

"Help!" The explorer Corona Wottley sat up in bed, running her long fingers through her carroty curls as she did so.

"That's funny!" she cried aloud. "That's very strange. Was that someone calling for help?" Her head was swimming with visions of ice and snow. "Albino penguins!" she exclaimed. "It's ages since I wondered about that colony of albino penguins. There were lots of stories about it, but no one has ever found out if it really exists. And what about the lost ship… what was it called? Yes! *The Riddle*! I haven't thought about *The Riddle* for years either. Why not? Bonniface Sapwood may have given up searching for it, the great big wimp, but that doesn't mean everyone else has to give up. If I set out now – immediately, if not sooner – and if I am strong and brave and determined, I might be the explorer who finds *The Riddle*. And I could look for the albino penguins at the same time. Suppose I found *The Riddle* and the white penguins too. *That* would show Bonniface Sapwood he isn't the only Antarctic explorer in the world."

She leaped out of bed and began to do a few warming-up exercises to get herself fit for the Antarctic, where warming-up exercises are particularly important.

CHAPTER 4

The Second Cry for Help

"Help!" The second ghost cry flew over the great Southern Ocean just as the first had done, and found the same country made up of islands. And at last the second cry found an ear that had been waiting for just such a cry, without quite knowing what it was waiting for. While the beautiful explorer, Corona Wottley, was beginning her exercises, an eye was opening in a mansion high on a hill in the middle of the business area of a great city... an eye so dark with black thoughts and wickedness you couldn't tell where the iris left off and the peering pupil began.

That eye stared up at a ceiling painted white – white as paper, white as snow – a ceiling that glittered from time to time with sharp little rainbows. Then, on the other side of the long nose, a second black eye opened, too, and these two eyes stared up at the points of rainbow glitter, a little sleepily at first but then sharply, and (within a second) more sharply still. Below those eyes, below the nose, there was a movement. A mouth began curving in a long, thin smile... a smile so cruel and greedy that it couldn't really count as a smile even if it did turn up at the ends.

The owner of that smile sat up in bed. He was wearing black pyjamas with diamond buttons. His sheets were made of black silk. His blankets were spun from the finest black wool, and his quilt was made from the skins of rare, coal-black foxes. And, though the ceiling was so white and glittering, the walls of his bedroom were made out of polished ebony. So he was cuddled and contained by darkness.

Directly opposite the end of his bed a huge framed map hung on the wall, and any explorer worth his salt would have been able to tell at a casual glance that it was the map of the Antarctic.

"*The Riddle!*" the man in black pyjamas murmured to himself. "Why haven't I thought of *The Riddle* for such a long time? I suppose with all those diamonds Grandaddy stole (and which came to me when he died, ha! ha!) I haven't really needed to remember it. But that cry I just dreamed — that cry of *Help!* — has reminded me all over again. Of course, I've still got plenty of those diamonds left over," (here he looked up at his glittering ceiling) "but a man can always do with more. Besides, Grandaddy may not have brought them all back with him, and if he didn't, it's my sacred duty to search for any that he might have left behind him. Yes! *The Riddle* must be found. It will be found. But who can I get to find it for me — because a delicate man like me can't go turning the Antarctic upside down. A man like me needs someone *else* to do all the actual searching. I hate walking in snow. Now who? Who?

"Aha! I have it. Bonniface Sapwood! Just the man. Now that I've remembered *The Riddle*, Bonniface Sapwood must be made to think about it all over again. He's been looking after those wretched children of his for long enough! I'll get him going, and he can do all the hard exploring work while I keep an eye on him. And if he *should* find *The Riddle*, or left-over diamonds, or anything like that, I'll be able to step in and take over. Oh! and what about that apprentice explorer he once had in his team? What was her name? Corona Something? I might just remind her too. It's good to have people chasing one another along. It saves you the trouble of having to chase them yourself. And everyone knows Antarctic explorers just love racing one another from place to place.

"Now, what else? Ah yes! A few explosions might be useful somewhere along the line, so I'll get in touch with that strange firm, Explosions Ltd. I hear the men who run it — the Tambo brothers — are good at explosions, and at wickedness too, a useful combination. Oh, how wonderful it is to be rich and clever! And how wonderful it is to lie in bed admiring myself. It's a pity I can't do it all day. But no! I'm too clever to do that. I must get up and get going! Where's that telephone?"

CHAPTER 5

The Third Cry of Help

That third cry of "Help!" had found an ear that let it in, and was winding its way into yet another sleeping head.

"I'm coming!" Bonniface Sapwood called aloud, tossing like a ship in a storybook sea as he spoke. The sound of his own voice woke him up and he lay on his back, gasping and goggling and trying to remember just what had woken him.

"That's funny!" he mumbled. "I thought I heard someone calling for help."

But his room was full of peaceful, yellow sunshine, and he could hear the distant voices of his children drifting in from the lawn. As he lay there blinking and mumbling, the telephone beside his bed let out a shrill cry. Bonniface jumped as if he had been stabbed, then grabbed the receiver. He usually began the day by yawning and stretching — something he was good at — but this morning, with the ghostly word "Help!" still echoing in his head, he felt too sharp — too *adventurous* — for even a single yawn.

"Bonniface Sapwood!" he announced down the phone, almost expecting to hear someone shouting for help at the other end. But there was no shouting.

"Is it really *you*, Bonniface," said an oily voice. "The great Bonniface? The Antarctic explorer who *almost* discovered the long lost *Riddle* some years ago?"

"Who is this?" demanded Bonniface crossly. "I was just working out an important dream and you've interrupted me."

"Never mind who I am," said the voice. "I am a secret admirer. That should be enough for you."

It was almost enough. Bonniface relaxed and smiled, pleased to think he had a secret admirer. The voice went on.

"I thought you should know that Corona Wottley (that *other* famous Antarctic explorer) decided (about twenty minutes ago) to visit the Antarctic once more."

"She is probably going to do more penguin research," said Bonniface. "She is very sound on penguins."

"I was just talking to her on the phone, and she is already packing her thermal underwear. She was boasting a little bit, I'm sorry to say — boasting that she would be the one to discover the lost *Riddle!*" said the oily voice.

Bonniface jumped as if he had been stung.

"How can she?" he cried. "I'm the one with the map — well, not a map, exactly. But I'm the one with ideas. I'm the one who nearly found it last time. And only five minutes ago I decided to set out and search for it all over again."

"Five minutes ago?" asked the oily voice. It chuckled. Somehow that chuckle had a very dark sound about it. "Five minutes is already a long time ago when it comes to an Antarctic race."

"Corona Wottley won't find *The Riddle!*" shouted Bonniface. "She's only a junior explorer. I should know, because I'm the one who gave her her first exploring lessons. Anyhow, as it happens, I'm leaving for the Antarctic myself. I know it's nearly Christmas, but I've been at home for four Christmases now, and besides, my children have Daffodil, our housekeeper, to look after them, so they'll be OK for a little while. And think how proud of me they'll be when I come home in triumph. It'll be a wonderful present for them."

He slammed the phone down and leaped to his feet, so excited that just for a moment he found himself dancing on the spot.

"Tonight will be too late!" he muttered to himself, looking at his watch. "I must go immediately!" he cried. "Or even sooner! No one must find the lost *Riddle* but me."

CHAPTER 6
On the Trampoline

Up and down... up and down... the three Sapwood children were out on the big blue trampoline, all enjoying a bit of early-morning bouncing while the early-morning blackbirds sang. They were having fun. As usual, Edward and Sophie were trying to out-bounce one another. Edward zoomed up, turning a somersault as he did so and feeling like a spaceman on a low-gravity planet. It seemed like practice for space travel and Edward longed to be a space traveller. In fact he was writing a science fiction novel just to go on with, and felt that bouncing on the trampoline was good practice for science fiction as well as space travel.

As Edward zoomed up, Sophie was zapping down. Boing! She hit the trampoline. Up she went, high into the air while Edward zapped down. It was all zap-and-zoom, zap-and-zoom with Sophie and Edward. Meanwhile, to one side of the big blue trampoline, Hotspur did a few little-kid-bum-bounces. He was a beautiful child — everyone said so — with black curls and long black lashes fringing big, blue eyes, but he was slightly strange as well. He was four years old, but had never said a word that anyone could understand. Mind you, he had plenty to say, but he sang and squawked and quacked and crowed and cawed and cooed and clucked and cackled. The trees close to the trampoline were crowded with sparrows and blackbirds all listening intently to Hotspur whistling and chirping as he did his bum-bounces.

Higher! Higher! Higher! went Edward. Higher! went Sophie! Higher, and then higher still! It felt wonderful.

"I'm going into orbit!" cried Edward, turning his usual somersault at the top of his bounce, then diving down again. He was longing to take notes for his science fiction adventure book, but it is hard to take notes when you are actually bouncing. It would be too easy to stick a pen in your eye.

"I can see Daffodil cooking breakfast!" Sophie sang, shooting up past him.

"I almost looked in at Dad's bedroom window that time," Edward boasted a moment later.

"And I *am* looking through Dad's bedroom window," Sophie shouted another moment later. "He's on the phone."

They kept on shouting cheerfully to one another as they zapped and zoomed.

"He's just slammed the phone down…" cried Edward.

"…looking excited…" screamed Sophie

"…rushing to the wardrobe…" (Edward)

"…dragging out his explorer clothes…" (Sophie)

"…his explorer clothes *and* his brown suitcase," Edward exclaimed. "Wow!"

"Oh-oh!" Sophie and Edward groaned in chorus as they accidentally bounced on top of one another. "This means trouble." But it wasn't their collision they were groaning about.

Off to one side, Hotspur whistled in apprehension and every bird in every nearby tree joined in too.

CHAPTER 7
Mukluk Kissing

Bonniface was packing quickly. Explorers are good packers. Quickly, quickly he packed seven pairs of underpants, one pair for each day of the week. Quickly, quickly he pulled on his favourite red thermal underwear, then lovingly folded his second-best blue thermal underwear and pushed it in beside his underpants. He packed his long johns (top and bottom), his second-best long johns, his woollen shirts (one red, one blue and one green) and his best explorer's padded waistcoat made of polypropylene.

"*I'll be cosy, I'll be clean, in my polypropylene,*" he sang as he folded this splendid garment. On top of his waistcoat, he packed woollen outer socks, vapour-barrier liner socks and a pair of thin polar-fleeced socks to go inside the other two. He packed sweaters, a fleecy inner jacket, an outer survival jacket, three balaclavas and a neck gaiter (which covered the part of his neck where his collar left off and his balaclava began). He also packed inner gloves, outer windproof mitts, sunglasses and snow goggles.

"But what about my feet?" he cried aloud, and began a feverish search, tossing mere sandals and sneakers left and right in his desperation. "Where are my fleecy salopettes? Where, oh where, are my mukluks?"

Shoes flew out behind him in all directions.

"Aha!" he cried in rapture a mere moment later. "Mukluks! My mukluks! Marvellous!"

Soaring up from the trampoline and looking through the window yet again, Sophie saw her father hugging two tall, tough, hard-and-heavy, laced-up, bright blue boots, especially made for walking in snow. She saw him plant smacking kisses on either shiny toe.

"Dad's kissing his mukluks," she cried as she plunged back to the trampoline.

"Uh-oh!" cried Edward, shooting up to see for himself. "Mukluk kissing means trouble. Not just *ordinary* trouble either. Mukluk kissing means *real* trouble."

Little Hotspur gave the cry of a particularly worried thrush.

But then all three children fell down and began rolling around on the trampoline, giggling their heads off. Something exciting was about to happen and, naturally, they loved excitement.

CHAPTER 8

Two Different Careers

Bonniface Sapwood grabbed his passport, some spare money and his notebook, along with various lists and maps which he then packed safely. He unlocked the safe in the corner of his room and took out a covered green folder filled with maps and pages covered with scribbles and question marks.

"Ready to go!" he cried happily, and danced downstairs.

Sophie and Edward were trying to tell little Hotspur what was going on. It was hard to know if he could understand them, but they told him just the same.

"Dad's packed his terminal underwear!" cried Sophie.

"Thermal, not terminal," Edward said. "Get it right!"

"Terminal means the end of something, and it might be the end of Dad," argued Sophie. "It nearly was, last time."

Hotspur crowed like a rooster. Rooster voices answered him from backyards all over the city.

"Hey, what will Daffodil say?" asked Edward beginning to bounce again.

"You already know what she'll say," cried Sophie.

"*Who's going to look after the kids?*" the two of them cried together, and they began laughing again. Only Hotspur looked uncertain.

"Don't worry, Hotspur," Sophie declared. "We'll look after ourselves."

"We always do," agreed Edward. "We've had to, haven't we? I mean, Dad's done his best, but we're the clever ones." And he began bouncing high... high... maybe higher than he had ever bounced before.

"Edward's going into orbit," shouted Sophie,

looking up at him in admiration. "He's a distant planet."

Inside the house, Bonniface Sapwood, faithful brown suitcase in hand, came thundering downstairs in his mukluks.

"What's for breakfast?" he cried joyously.

But his housekeeper, Daffodil, was standing at the door with her own suitcase (a pink one) packed and bulging beside her. They stared at each other in horror.

"Where do you think you're going?" they cried together, pointing at one another's suitcases.

"I'm an explorer, remember!" Bonniface declared. "I'm going to find *The Riddle*. That's always been my dream."

"But I've got a chance of dancing in a Christmas ballet," Daffodil declared right back at him. "And that's always been *my* dream. I've been practising for weeks."

"Who's going to look after the kids?" they shouted simultaneously, glaring across the kitchen at each other.

Out on the trampoline, Edward, Sophie and Hotspur were listening, rolling on the trampoline, and laughing crazily.

"They're *your* kids!" said Daffodil at last.

"But listen..." begged Bonniface. "I've just had a new theory about where we might find the wreck of The Riddle. Daffodil, I must find that lost ship before anyone else does."

"It's just an old ship," said Daffodil. "It probably won't ever sail again."

"It's The Riddle!" yelled Bonniface. "The First Mate, Escher Black, led the crew to safety after the ice closed in on it, but that's only part of the story. If I find The Riddle, I'll find the ship's logbook, and then I'll know exactly what happened and why. I'll write a book about it all. It'll be a bestseller and someone is bound to make a film of it. Maybe even a ballet — a mukluk ballet!"

"Listen!" said Daffodil. "I told you when I came to work here that I'd have to go when I had a chance to dance. I thought you understood. Well, you said you did."

"But I've already packed my thermal underwear and my best polypropylene waistcoat," said Bonniface. "Be reasonable!"

"And I have packed my tights and my tutu," said Daffodil. She leaped to straighten the curtain at the kitchen window — a leap so graceful that Bonniface was distracted by her footwork and failed to see the expression of great cunning which crossed her face.

"Oh well, perhaps I will be reasonable," she cooed, turning round again, "Eat up your fried egg and we'll argue about it later."

The fried egg certainly smelled good.

But out on the trampoline, Edward, Sophie and even Hotspur had all seen that expression of cunning cross Daffodil's face.

"Shall we tell?" asked Sophie, while Hotspur twittered like a fantail. Fantails came out of the garden trees and twittered back at him.

"Let's just see what happens next," said Edward. "That's what you do in stories. I might take a few notes."

A writer never knows just what is going to turn out to be useful.

CHAPTER 9

The Treachery of a Housekeeper

What happened next, in this particular story, was that their housekeeper sneaked out of the back door. She ran over to the trampoline, holding a finger across her lips. Then she took the finger away and kissed Edward, Sophie and Hotspur, but very quietly. (She usually gave them great smacking, musical kisses like cymbals being flicked together). Then she vaulted lightly over the garden wall with the grace of a trained ballet dancer, and slid into her car — a red 'Snifitzu' — which was parked in front of the garage.

Gently and silently, she put it into reverse; gently and silently she took off the handbrake and coasted down the sloping drive. When she hit the main road (after looking carefully both ways), she took off like a rocket.

Three minutes later Bonniface called out, asking where the tomato sauce was.

Four minutes later he got up and began to search the house for tomato sauce, calling Daffodil's name as he did so. His voice echoed in empty rooms.

Five minutes later a howl of fury and anguish rang out in the Sapwood kitchen.

CHAPTER 10

A Startling Idea for a Devoted Father

"How could she do this to me?" Bonniface complained bitterly. He mopped up the last of his egg with the last of his toast – toast he had been forced to make himself.

"It's nearly Christmas," said Sophie, for the children had come in from the trampoline to comfort their father. "You could put off going to the Antarctic until after Christmas."

"You don't understand," cried Bonniface. "I've just had a dream. I heard a mysterious voice. 'Help!' it cried. Now, a lot of people would be confused by a voice calling 'Help!' but not me. I *knew* — knew for sure — that it was an Antarctic voice. And it was calling *me*! ME! And it wanted me *now*! And not only that, I had the strangest feeling that I knew where it was calling from. I suddenly remembered an inlet — the Inlet of Ghosts, they called it — which people talked about without quite knowing whether it was really there, and I woke up with a sudden new theory about where I might find *The Riddle*, so..."

"You'll have to take us with you," interrupted Edward. "I'd rather go to another planet, but going to the Antarctic might be a sort of science fiction practice." Hotspur gave the cry of an excited goose.

"Antarctic explorers never take their kids exploring with them," shouted Bonniface. "Scott didn't! Shackleton didn't! Amundsen? No way!"

"It might have been more fun for them if they had," said Edward.

Bonniface crunched his toast thoughtfully. Slowly, his expression changed till suddenly he thumped the kitchen table with his clenched fist. He thumped it so hard that the bottle of tomato sauce leaped high in the air.

"You're right !" he cried. "Why should I copy Scott and Shackleton? Why shouldn't I be the first explorer to take my children with me? I *want* to look after you kids. I *long* to try out my new *Riddle* theory. And I absolutely *need* to answer that cry of 'Help!' I'll do all three things at once. It's settled. We'll all go south!"

"Hooray!" shouted Edward and Sophie, while Hotspur chortled like a happy magpie. "We'll pack at once."

"You will need thermal underwear," their father shouted after them.

"You gave us some last Christmas," Sophie called back. "And the Christmas before that."

Bonniface smiled proudly, thinking what a good father he had been.

"What I really wanted was a reflecting telescope," Edward muttered. Still, it was no use worrying about past disappointments.

"And do you have polypropylene jerkins?" Bonniface shouted again.

"You gave us jerkins *and* jackets for our birthdays," Edward's voice came back faintly. "We have complete sets of explorer clothes! And mukluks! Even Hotspur has mukluks – though he really wanted trainer skates."

Hotspur! Bonniface suddenly frowned. The older children might be useful. They could cook, do up their own jerkins and jackets and mukluks. But Hotspur!

"Perhaps we should send Hotspur to Granny's," he suggested. But this suggestion made Hotspur squawk like an angry seagull.

"Dad!" cried Sophie. "We can't leave Hotspur behind. I know he's little, but every little helps."

Oh well, thought Bonniface, there wouldn't be too much work in looking after anyone as small as Hotspur. He ran to his fax machine, planning to contact Scott Base on Ross Island, on the very edge of the great, frozen continent. He wanted to let them know he was coming and to order a particularly good skiddoo — a sort of Antarctic motor-sledge.

"It must be a state-of-the-art skiddoo!" he muttered to himself. "Nothing but the best will do. And when they hear that I'm bringing the kids, they'll make sure that I get the very best. After all, it's nearly Christmas. They'll want the children to be safe as well as happy at Christmas. There might, after all, be great advantages in taking the kids with me."

CHAPTER 11

Unexpected Air Travel

The Sapwood children always travelled by plane when they visited their grandmother. They were used to airline seatbelts, and looked forward to free aeroplane lollies. But the inside of the Hercules aircraft (which was waiting to take explorers and scientists to Antarctica) took them by surprise. For travelling by Hercules turned out to be rather like flying in a second-hand-clothes-and-general-junk shop. There were seats, of course (you didn't have to stand all the way to the Antarctic), but they weren't like ordinary aeroplane seats. They were made of a curious orange webbing and they ran around the edge of the Hercules cabin. You strapped yourself in and sat there, staring inwards towards the middle of the plane. And down the middle of that cabin ran tall racks on which people hung coats and slung luggage. A man in an orange-coloured overall and headphones moved around, handing out plastic bags. Sophie thought perhaps they were being given large bags full of sweets, or something to be sick into, but it turned out he was handing ear-muffs to everyone.

Of course, the Hercules was full of people all going to Antarctica and, while they waited for the journey to start, Bonniface pointed them out to his children... helicopter pilots, geologists, penguin experts, drill-operators, and so on.

"It's almost as good as going to another planet," Edward whispered to Sophie, who nodded in a rather distracted way. As she had climbed on to the plane, suddenly the pendant, hidden under layers of warm clothes, had shifted against her skin as if it were startled. She had the odd idea that, even through layers of jerseys and jackets, it had recognised someone, and that somewhere in the Hercules, someone smiling and cheerful had also recognised – not the invisible pendant, perhaps, but certainly the whole Sapwood family, and had stopped smiling. Sophie peered around anxiously, but there wasn't a single person looking disturbed, dismayed, or disgusted by the sight of a famous explorer taking three children on a dangerous expedition.

The Sapwood family settled down on the webbing seats and strapped themselves in. A merry crowd of Antarctic helicopter pilots were settling themselves opposite, and singing a fine old Antarctic helicopter-pilot's song.

"Oh, let us meander
Out over Lake Vanda
Where we'll take a gander
At prospects of snow.

Or we may be nosier
And make for Cape Crozier
The prospect is rosier
At forty below!"

Sophie touched the front of her jacket under which the pendant was nestling – a warm tear just over her heart. Then something caught her eye. A cluster of bright orange waterproof coats with hoods was hanging almost opposite her, billowing out over the end of an empty section of seating, and below these coats she saw a pair of mukluks that looked as if they might have real feet in them. It was hard to be sure. But, feet or not, these mukluks were particularly interesting in themselves. They were blue, and decorated with gold and silver stars. Sophie liked the look of them. She liked the idea of someone taking starry strides across the Antarctic. But was there someone concealed by those coats... someone sleeping or, perhaps, hiding under them? It was hard to tell.

"There aren't many windows," muttered Edward interrupting Sophie's thoughts.

"Where's the air hostess?" she asked her father.

"There aren't any air hostesses on an Antarctic Hercules," cried Bonniface scornfully. "We're not tourists!"

But just then the Hercules started up, and the cabin immediately became far too noisy for any of them to hear a word. Bonniface hastily slid ear-muffs on to Hotspur's head, and gestured to Edward and Sophie to put on their ear-muffs as well. He pointed at the bag of books dangling from the rack that ran down the middle of the plane, meaning that they were both to read quietly because it was going to be too hard to talk during the flight.

Edward pulled a pen and a little notebook out of his pocket and scribbled away, busily taking notes for his future famous novel, but Sophie sat still until the plane had levelled out. Then, when other people began standing up and stretching and wandering around, Sophie stood, stretched and wandered too, until she found a small round window at the very end of the cabin. Standing on tiptoes, she peered out eagerly.

There wasn't much to see. A rippling carpet of greyish cloud rolled out under the Hercules and, staring ahead, Sophie found they were flying into a blueness that seemed to go on forever. She gazed into that blueness, filling her head with it, and suddenly she glimpsed, from the very corner of her eye, something flying a little above them. Some hawk? Some high-flying albatross? No, thought Sophie, squinting upwards. No bird ever flew quite as high as the Hercules was flying.

She peered even harder, pressing her nose against the glass. Yes! There, one whole layer of the sky above them – say, a thousand feet – was another plane… a black one. It looked a little threatening, thought Sophie, almost as if it were secretly planning to swoop down on them.

But the Hercules flew steadily onwards, and Sophie soon lost sight of the black plane altogether.

CHAPTER 12

Wicked Plans in Black Planes

Funnily enough, a thousand feet above the Sapwood family, in that very black plane, someone was telling two people an Antarctic story. However, the long cabin of the black plane was entirely different from the cabin of the Hercules. Its soft seats were covered in black velvet and there were television screens set about the walls. You could watch several videos at the same time.

At the far end of the cabin stood a bar where orange juice was served, or champagne, or whatever you felt like drinking, and through the windows all passengers had wonderful, stretching views of sky and cloud. What's more, this cabin was not only warm but quiet. There was no need for any of the three people in the cabin to wear ear-muffs or mukluks or any compulsory Antarctic clothing. Indeed, one of the three men was wearing black shorts and black sandals, because this man (his name was Rancid Swarthy) loved to cloak himself in darkness, even in mid-summer.

At that moment Rancid Swarthy was highly delighted with his velvet chairs and his champagne, but mostly, he was delighted with himself. He longed to smile broadly, but he was a man who had to be careful when it came to smiling, because even his very sweetest smile (his Number Six smile) made people uneasy. As for his Number Two smile — that one was so mean and threatening that when he used it, people crouched down with their hands over their eyes. And he only used his Number One smile when he was looking at himself in the mirror. He was the only person in the world who could bear it. It was like a secret weapon.

So he sat there struggling with himself, for though he was longing to grin like a wolverine, and to boast about his riches and his cleverness, he knew that a boasting man says too much. He must be careful and cunning.

"I'm searching for a ship," he told the two men opposite him. "It was lost in the Antarctic during my grandfather's day. You may have heard of it. It was called *The Riddle*. My grandfather, Escher Black, was *The Riddle's* First Mate."

"Do you want me to explode this ship when you find it?" asked the bigger of his two companions, but in rather an absent-minded tone of voice. Rancid frowned. This man was not paying proper attention. Indeed, he seemed far more interested in fooling around with something that looked like a firework.

"If your grandfather was called 'Black', how is it that you are called 'Swarthy'?" asked the other man, who did seem to be listening intently. His name was Whizzy Tambo and he was the secretary of the company, Explosions Ltd. At least he seemed to be full of the deepest respect for Rancid Swarthy. Reassured, Rancid relaxed once more and went on with his story.

"My grandfather, Escher Black, renamed himself 'Swarthy' when he grew rich and successful," he explained with quiet dignity. "'Swarthy' sounds so sinuous and stylish…" ("It does! It does!" agreed Whizzy Crambo.) "…and it means, more or less, the same thing as 'Black'."

At this moment there was a small explosion. The big man had set off his firework. It leaped into the air, broke into sparks and fell on the cabin carpet. The man who had set it off quickly stamped on it. Since the carpet was so very dark, it was hard to tell if any spark had actually burned a hole.

Then the firework man looked over at Rancid Swarthy and grinned. "Just practising!" he said.

Rancid smiled back at him. He used a Number Three smile – one that usually frightened people and made them quiet and obedient. But it seemed to have no effect on that third man who swelled up in his black velvet chair, looking extremely pleased with himself. This big man was Whizzy Tambo's brother, Crambo Tambo – his little brother, which was a bit of a joke since he was actually twice as big as Whizzy.

"This is *not* the time for explosions!" said Rancid Swarthy, speaking very quietly but managing to sound fearsome. He was highly pleased with his own terrorising skill but, to his surprise, Crambo answered back.

"Any time is the time for an explosion," he declared. Rancid could hardly believe it. Crambo was close to contradicting him.

"And just being honest, Sir," Whizzy put in quickly, "you *have* brought us along because you *do*

57

want us to blow someone up, don't you? I mean my brother and I *are* Explosions Ltd."

"Huge explosions are our specialty," added Crambo in a pious voice. "Dangerous work! We must practise constantly."

"But not up here," said Rancid. "It's such a long way to fall."

"This Escher Black, your noble ancestor who changed his name, was he the one who made the family fortune?" Whizzy asked, snatching up his glass and slurping his champagne.

"He started it off," admitted Rancid Swarthy slowly, wondering, just for a moment, if he had done the right thing in employing Explosions Ltd. But of course he had! He was not a man who made mistakes.

"Do go on," said Whizzy quickly. "I am fascinated by your tale."

Rancid felt easy once more. After all, if the Tambos *should* get out of hand he could always smile his Number One smile – his most terrible smile – at them. That always worked. Sitting forward, he cleared his throat, preparing to boast a little.

"Well, Escher Black was not only an explorer; he was a collector too. For instance, he brought a great collection of stones back from the Antarctic with him. Wonderful stones! He treasured every one of them."

The Tambo brothers looked astonished. You could tell at a glance that they would have thrown all stones from the Antarctic away – probably aiming them at nearby penguins or seals.

"Kept a lot of stones?" Whizzy Tambo asked uneasily. "Wasn't that a little odd – a shade *eccentric* – Sir?"

"Mind you, stones can be interesting once you set a bomb off under them!" Crambo Tambo sounded suddenly enthusiastic.

Rancid smiled again, his Number Three smile, which was so unpleasant that Whizzy pretended he had a bit of grit in his eyes and began blinking and pulling his upper eyelid over the lower one. But he did not stop listening. A smile like that had to mean something important.

"As it turned out, most of the stones were diamonds," Rancid said casually, "so it's just as well he didn't throw them away or even explode them, isn't it?"

"Diamonds!" cried both Tambo brothers greedily. Whizzy stopped holding down his eyelid, and even Crambo began listening properly at last. Rancid was totally in charge once more.

"If we do a bit of exploding out on the ice, are *we* likely to find diamonds ourselves?" asked Whizzy eagerly.

"There is to be no exploding unless I say so," replied Rancid. "Understand this! I will take a hundred dollars off your fee for every unauthorised explosion."

"Oh, you're a hard man," cried Whizzy in the sort of fawning voice Rancid loved to hear.

"My grandfather, Escher Black, has always been my model," he went on, relaxing in his chair again. "He sold a few diamonds, set up in business, and soon he was being really helpful to poor, struggling bank managers, bomb experts like yourselves, and other needy people. And he trained me to do good in the same way."

"Oh, what a wonderful man!" said Whizzy, nodding his head, but Crambo was already a little bored. He slid another firework out of his pocket and looked at it wistfully.

"Mind you, nobody's perfect. He did make one bad mistake," admitted Rancid with a deep sigh. "He never told either my father, or me, exactly where he had found those diamonds in the first place. I have always been curious about that. And I rather think that if we find the ship on which he was sailing at the time – that missing ship, The Riddle – we might find a few diamond clues. The ship's logbook, for example, might well be full of useful information. Just think!

Wouldn't it be fun to know exactly where those diamonds had been found?"

"Wonderful fun!" cried Whizzy, raising his glass to toast Rancid.

There was sudden suspicious bang from Crambo's direction.

"Yeah! Wonderful fun," Crambo promptly cried, nodding his head and hastily treading something into the black carpet. "That's not an explosion," he added, looking over at Rancid. "Well, not what I'd call an explosion. When I *really* explode something there's absolutely no doubt about it." True enthusiasm crept into his voice and he flexed his muscles. Rancid gritted his teeth, holding back his most terrible smiles.

"It is true," he said carefully, "that I may need to explode a few things in the Antarctic. Even an explorer or two! You have those explosions to look forward to."

"Hooray!" cheered both Tambo brothers, but Crambo actually went on thinking — something that didn't happen very often.

"A bit earlier," he said frowning, "you mentioned this particular explorer who we are in pursuit of… what was his name?" He immediately answered himself. "Bonniface Sapwood! Now, do you reckon he might lead us to those diamonds?"

Rancid nodded. "He just might."

"Right!" agreed Whizzy. "And I suppose, if he *does* find that *Riddle* we'll drop down on him so you can lay claim to the ship's logbook — or any spare diamonds that might be lying around. After all, they *are* really yours, aren't they? I mean it was your grandfather who found them in the first place."

"If Bonniface should find *The Riddle*, any logbooks or spare diamonds will certainly belong to me," agreed Rancid Swarthy, beaming at his companions, though this time he was using a mere Number Five smile, easy to bear as long as the person being smiled at didn't look too closely.

"But what if he argues? I read somewhere that Antarctic explorers can be very quarrelsome," said Crambo, absent-mindedly bending his silver spoon into a horseshoe shape.

Rancid's Number Five smile changed to a Number Three. Whizzy quickly looked out of the window, but Crambo took no notice at all.

"Bonniface Sapwood has his children with him," Rancid sighed. "He wouldn't want to see his children exploded, would he? Even if he is silly enough to argue with us, I'm sure he won't argue for long."

"We can always explode them after he's passed the logbook over," said Crambo.

"I'm glad we understand one another," said Rancid.

He lay back in his black chair in which parts of him became almost invisible. Lounging there, he looked entirely at ease with himself. Yet, secretly, something was troubling him. Why was it that Crambo Tambo had seemed to take no notice of his wicked smiles? That was bothersome. I might be forced to use my Number One smile on Crambo, thought Rancid. That will certainly pull him into line.

Then, as Rancid lay there brooding, a spark — just a little one — leaped from between Crambo's hands. There was a crack like a whip and for the third time Crambo quickly wiped his foot over something smouldering in the black carpet. Rancid took a breath, and began a Number One smile as he turned towards Crambo. However, he was interrupted.

"Look!" cried Whizzy quickly. "There on the horizon! Land ho! Do you see it, Sir? The Antarctic is in sight."

CHAPTER 13

Getting There

"Land ho! The Antarctic is in sight," Edward cried —
and so it was.

Little Hotspur must have heard the word 'land' in
his dreams, for he woke up and ran to join them at
the round window. Edward lifted him up; Sophie
pointed sideways and Hotspur gave a strange
whistling cry. "We've been travelling for hours and

hours," exclaimed Sophie, "and it's still daylight."

"Of course!" Edward shouted back scornfully. "It's close to Christmas, isn't it? Midsummer in this part of the world! It's going to be daylight all the time in the Antarctic."

"Oh yes," nodded Sophie, suddenly remembering. Then her expression changed. "No bedtime! Great!"

"Don't forget that Santa Claus only brings presents to sleeping people," yelled Edward. "Hey! We'd better get back and strap ourselves in before the plane lands."

And, strapped into their windowless, webbing seats, they landed safely. The plane thudded down softly, slid forward, and came at last to a standstill. As people leaped to their feet, struggling into their survival jackets and pulling hoods over heads, Bonniface bounced up too, like a man who expects to be first off the plane. But then he realised that Hotspur would need help with his mukluks and zippers (though he was doing very well for someone aged only four). Bonniface sighed a little impatiently, but he helped Hotspur just as a good father should, nobly allowing other people to climb down from the Hercules ahead of him. At last, hung all over with various bags and packs and carrying Hotspur, he followed Edward and Sophie down the steps to stand, at last, on Antarctic snow.

Bonniface took a breath of deep fulfilment. Then he nudged Edward and Sophie to keep them moving, for Edward and Sophie were standing as if frozen – not with cold, but with amazement.

There in front of them, rising out of the snow, were long green sheds. Sophie and Edward could see snow tractors along with a fine flagpole, its flag dancing cheerfully and sometimes cracking like a whip. Directly ahead of them two lines of different coloured trucks were parked nose to nose. Big machines lumbered by looking busy; someone shot past, driving something that reminded Edward of a speedboat, but which he knew to be one of the skiddoos his father always spoke of with such longing and respect. A black helicopter was waiting on one of the helicopter pads, while yet another helicopter – a green and silver Antarctic dragonfly – throbbed like a beating heart, and then lifted into the air. Yet, for all its busy, bright machines, the whole big base seemed to be laid out on the snow like a toy, for beyond the helicopters, their landing pads, the bulldozers, skiddoos and the great green sheds, rose a strange white land, so huge and cold that its hugeness and coldness melted into each other and became single and magical.

The dragonfly helicopter tilted away over the green roofs. It made a lot of noise and, somewhere beyond it, tractors were roaring too; yet the silence of the Antarctic arched over all sounds, pressing down on them, and making them seem childish and easy to forget. Of course, the children could hear everything that was going on, but they heard the silence even more. Under all Sophie's layers of clothes, the bone pendant leaped like a beating heart that has suddenly received good news.

Now the children were glad of their thermal underwear, their long johns, their two pairs of trousers, their polypropylene waistcoats and fleecy-lined survival jackets, not to mention their mitts and mukluks.

"This is just the beginning for us," said Bonniface Sapwood, sounding more at home in the Antarctic than he did when was at home. "First we're going to Shed Ten – that's over there – to get our skiddoo. I've ordered the very best skiddoo available in the whole Antarctic… a true state-of-the-art skiddoo. It will be able to skim over the snow, light as a snowy petrel. Of course, most skiddoos are really just for one person, but they can pull trailers so you kids will be able to ride on our trailer behind me. We'll start at once, and make for a particular snow hut I remember where we'll camp for the— well, not for the night because there's no night at this time of the year, but we'll have a bit of a rest anyway. You know, I'm glad I brought you with me. It's fun to think I'm sharing adventures with you." He sounded a little surprised, but he did sound truly happy.

"What are those flags for?" asked Edward, pointing beyond the sheds and tractors. A long, long line of coloured flags led off over the snow, marching on and on until the whiteness took over and it became impossible to be sure if the flags were still there.

"Those flags show us where the ground is safe," explained Bonniface. "If we follow those flags we won't fall into any crevasses. Of course, once we get beyond the flags we'll have to be extra careful. But that's all right! I told them to pack an ice drill."

And, striding out boldly in his conquering mukluks, he led his children to Shed Ten.

Drawn up in front of the shed were – not one, but two skiddoos, both with covered trailers hitched on behind. One of them was a particularly beautiful skiddoo – a bright red in colour. Two men in red jackets and yellow overalls stood on either side of this elegant machine, looking with great pride at it.

"A four-seater skiddoo!" exclaimed Bonniface. "I've never heard of such a thing."

"Look at that instrument panel," exclaimed Edward in delight. "This skiddoo looks like a sort of little space ship."

"I asked for a state-of-the-art skiddoo," said Bonniface, "but I didn't expect anything quite as grand as this."

"Oh, we had a special message from Rancid Swarthy Industries saying you were to have every support," said one of the men in yellow overalls.

Bonniface blinked then beamed.

"That was kind of him," he said. "Of course, Rancid Swarthy's grandfather was First Mate on *The Riddle*, you know, so I suppose he takes an interest in Antarctic events." All the same, Bonniface sounded rather surprised.

"Swarthy Industries said you were to have the fastest skiddoo available," said the man, taking a notebook from his pocket and consulting it. "We've packed tents, a cell phone, sleeping bags, string, food, Sellotape, spare cans of skiddoo fuel, *extra* cans of skiddoo fuel, thermos flasks — everything you might need. Now, if you'll just sign here to show you've taken delivery..."

"Who's the blue skiddoo for?" asked Edward curiously.

"I think that must be for me," said a voice right behind them — a laughing voice that was somehow very sure of itself.

CHAPTER 14

A Skiddoo is Stolen

At the sound of that voice Bonniface whirled around. A figure, zipped up to the ears in a blue jacket and blue trousers was standing right behind him. It was hard to be sure (for the figure's face was mostly covered by snow goggles), but the children felt certain that the figure in blue was mocking Bonniface.

Then that figure pulled the hood of her survival

jacket back and pushed her sun goggles up. Edward, Sophie and Hotspur all immediately recalled the many gold-framed photographs of their father's exploring team, which hung up and down the stairs at home. This explorer was in most of them. She had a head covered in wild, carrot-coloured curls, big green eyes and a lopsided smile that made everyone she smiled at want to smile back at her. Certainly, Sophie couldn't help smiling back, shooting a quick glance at the newcomer's boots. Yes! Her mukluks were covered with gold and silver stars.

"Corona Wottley!" exclaimed Bonniface. "What are you doing here?"

"Bonniface, I am setting out to discover what happened to the lost *Riddle*," said Corona. She rested her pack on the back seat of the red skiddoo. "A voice called to me. 'Help!' it said. 'Help!' And for some reason I knew it was *The Riddle's* voice. I am going to find that doomed ship once and for all. I, Corona Wottley, am going to restore it to its true place in history."

"But I dreamed that cry for help too," shouted Bonniface. "I'll bet I dreamed it first, because I have had years and years of practice at Antarctic dreaming! And it gave me a new theory about where *The Riddle* might be. Corona, go and watch penguins! Find those albino birds that we used to hear rumours about! Only a highly experienced explorer is going to be able to locate The Riddle, and I'm the only highly experienced explorer here."

"But you might be too high and too experienced," said Corona. "What the discovery of The Riddle needs is a young explorer with a fresh, down-to-earth view of the ice."

"What it needs," yelled Bonniface, "is an explorer with a new skiddoo… a red skiddoo with state-of-the-art technology." And he looked over at the red skiddoo with pride.

"You are quite right," said Corona. And quick as a wink, she leaped into the driver's seat and turned the key. Her pack was already on the back seat. Off she flew, moving like a beam of red light as she reversed, then swung out in a half-circle and slid away at great speed. Bonniface sprang to stop her. He missed and ran after her, shouting as he ran. But he was carrying Hotspur, and Hotspur weighed him down. Too late! Corona Wottley was on her way, shooting past the tractors and past the sheds, making for the line of coloured flags that wound away over the snow into infinite, white distance.

CHAPTER 15
Off and Away At Last

Bonniface nearly had a fit. "She's pinched my skiddoo!" he yelled, shaking poor Hotspur in the heat of his fury. "She's got my supplies. Stop her!"

"She hasn't signed for that skiddoo either," said one of the men, looking concerned.

"Well, Mr Sapwood," said the other man, "the best thing you can do is to sign for this other skiddoo and take off after her. I'd go myself, but there's a plane – one of the Swarthy Industries fleet – about to land in a minute and… "

"And Swarthy Industries take all our attention," said the first man. "They pay for it in advance so… "

"But this blue skiddoo isn't state-of-the-art," cried Bonniface. "I ordered that super-computerised model… and don't forget, I did have the backing of the Swarthy Industries. They'd want you to help me."

"They'd want us to help *them* first," said the second man.

"Oh, come on, Dad," said Edward "Let's go. We kids can ride on the trailer, can't we? "

"We can tie ourselves on with all the bags and stuff," said Sophie. "We'll enjoy the fun of it." And Hotspur warbled like a magpie.

"Your kids show good sense," said one of the men in red approvingly. "I'd get after that skiddoo thief as quickly as possible."

The children helped Bonniface strap their packs under the yellow tarpaulin that took up most of the trailer, and then they all squeezed into a space in front of the packs while Bonniface leaped into the driver's seat of the blue skiddoo. Fortunately the motor started immediately and they shot away at a cracking pace, swinging around the end of a green shed and following the tracks that Corona had left behind her. People cheered and waved as they drove by. Within seconds, Boniface too was following the line of coloured flags.

"Wow! Great!" yelled Edward. "It's like being on a moon buggy."

But Bonniface couldn't help frowning. His noble *Riddle* adventure was turning into yet another undignified Antarctic race and, no doubt about it, Corona was off to a wonderful start.

There was a roar overhead... already another plane was coming in to land. Sophie watched it, at first with interest and then with a curious feeling that was just a little like fear. It was not a Hercules. It was a black ski-plane which slid over the snow in a furtive, slippery way. As it shot by, in a shower of freezing spray, a face looked out of the window and she glimpsed a truly horrible smile. She hastily looked away and read the small red letters running along its side.

"Swarthy Industries," she said aloud.

"Oh, them!" said Bonniface, in an absent-minded voice for, in spite of having had his red skiddoo hijacked by a junior explorer, he was beginning to enjoy himself. Even if you have been cheated out of a skiddoo that is rightfully yours, there is something wonderful about spinning out across Antarctic snow and seeing mountains ahead of you, beautiful as dreams yet somehow truer than dreams. Once you have seen those mountains there is no waking up from them. They are in your head for always.

As for Edward and Sophie, they were both now staring across a stretch of dark beach. Summer winds had beaten the snow back, revealing black sand and stones, curving away towards a distant headland. Embraced by this beach was yet another long curve (of broken ice this time), and beyond the ice, the sea spread like a great blue plain. *Old! Old! Old!* that Antarctic sea whispered to Sophie while, in the distance, on the other side of the sea, far, far beyond the black stones and the broken ice, Sophie could make out another distant blue-and-white shoreline marked with valleys, peaks and glaciers.

"It's like being on another planet," said Edward again.

"It's cold enough to freeze your nose off!" said Sophie. Indeed the cold was so fierce it seemed as if you should be able to fling your arms around it and wrestle with it, as you might with a bear.

The skiddoo motor kept up its chatter and snow shushed away on either side of them, but it was impossible to forget the silence, always there, just beyond the busy fringes of sound. Sometimes the land under the snow rose and fell, so that they shot up-over-then-down, up-over–then-down, and whenever this happened it felt as if the Antarctic was breathing beneath them. All three children yelled with pleasure and Bonniface cheered up even more. Sophie began to sing.

"If you feel blue, get on your skiddoo
And swiffle your way through the snow,
Skiddare to be bold even though it is cold
Skiddon't let it lay you low!
Skiddaddle along, singing a song
Skiddoodle what has to be done!
Your heart will skiddance at each fabulous chance
And skididdle-dee-dee at the fun."

After she had sung this song twice Edward was able to join in, while as for Hotspur, he sang like a lark, embroidering the edges of the song with the sort of whistling that has no beginning or end. After ten verses even Bonniface joined in the carolling as they whisked along, singing their hearts out, but always knowing that the silence, which was waiting all around them, would win out in the end.

"Dad, it is *so* beautiful," cried Sophie at last, and

Bonniface looked at her, smiling and surprised, as if she had just made him look at the Antarctic in a different way.

"It is," he agreed. "It really is."

CHAPTER 16

A Ghost with Problems

"I must remember! I must remember!"

On *The Riddle*, the ghost of Captain Cathcardo was standing as still as a frozen man. He had prowled around his ship many times by now, rather as if he were learning it by heart, and he was rather enjoying this patch of stillness which made him feel as if he were actually *part* of his ship. All the same, there were plenty of things he was still wondering about, and parts of a ship don't usually wonder about anything.

"I was a captain and now I am a ghost," he repeated dreamily. "I have lost my pendant and I can't leave The Riddle. How did all this happen?"

Captain Cathcardo found he couldn't remember anything useful. All the same he could feel all sorts of things going on in his head... coloured lines were winding and weaving in and out of each other. Look! There was a blue line and he traced it with pleasure because, for some reason, he felt as if it might be bringing him good luck. Not only that, the blue line seemed to be chasing after a carrot-coloured line which, for some reason, reminded him of the days when he was a dashing young explorer anxious to discover absolutely everything.

But what about that black skull-shaped smudge, which seemed to be chasing after both the blue and red lines and snapping its teeth all the way? There was something about that smudge which made the Captain's ghostly hair stand on end and give off sparks of eerie alarm. The blue line, the carroty one and the black skull-shaped patch all seemed to be swinging in his direction, acting out some sort of a story as they came towards him, but Captain Cathcardo couldn't quite make out what was happening in that story.

Someone is coming my way, he thought. I do know that. It feels as if my pendant is coming back to me. And it looks as if someone *else* is following it. Why? It might be because of those diamonds.

Diamonds!

The Captain was thunderstruck. He had remembered something new, and all without trying. He had found *diamonds*. He had climbed down (all on his own) into a pit of some kind. There had been water at the bottom of it – warm water! But here the Captain hesitated, pulled a face, and then began pacing again. Because how could there possibly be warm water in the Antarctic – a place where whole oceans freeze over? Yet, all the same, the water *had* been warm. He had definitely felt its warmth, even through his mukluks.

Captain Cathcardo clutched his poor head in dismay and rocked it from side to side. To his horror his whole head came off in his hands and he had to concentrate on putting it back again, so that his eyes looked more or less straight ahead once more. But even while his head was still rocking between his hands it was struggling to remember. You found diamonds, part of his melted memory told him. Hundreds of them – just lying around. Of course, they hadn't been cut and polished and glittering like the diamonds in a jeweller's window, but they were true diamonds for all that. A fortune in diamonds!

And the funny thing was, he thought (straightening his head just a little bit more), he hadn't been looking for diamonds. He had been looking for something else... something much more interesting than mere jewels. Captain Cathcardo's face suddenly brightened and his blueish light brightened too. Of course! He had been searching for meteorites. That had been part of his Antarctic research, though his old friend, Escher Black, had rather sneered at meteorites. But dear old Escher, bless his heart, had been a sailor not a scientist.

Most meteorites are small — no bigger than walnuts — but Captain Cathcardo had actually seen this one falling and it had been as big as a house. He found he could remember it quite clearly now, blazing down, down, down from outer space. For a dreadful moment it had even seemed that meteorite might hit *The Riddle*. How terrified poor old Escher Black had been. (Captain Cathcardo chuckled affectionately.) But it had missed them by a mile or two and had dived, blazing, into deep snow a little to the south.

Aha! Of course! That explained the melted snow and the warm water. Everything is simple when you remember properly. That meteor tried to hide, but I found it, thought the Captain triumphantly. I even walked on it while it was still warm. I took samples from it. I measured it. And I filled my pockets with the diamonds that were scattered over it. I bought most them back to The Riddle and after that... now, what happened after that? Is that why I am here, haunting this upper deck? And where is my good-luck charm – my pendant?

But then this ghostly presence glowed a little more brightly, standing there on the haunted ship in the haunted cave.

"I'm sure that pendant is coming back to me," murmured Captain Cathcardo. "I can feel someone carrying it in this direction. And once I have that pendant I might be able to get away from this frozen old Riddle. I might be set free. In the meantime, I'll concentrate on remembering everything I possibly can. Where was I? Oh yes! Diamonds! I found diamonds. I wonder what happened to them?"

CHAPTER 17
The End of the Road

Suddenly the line of flags ended. There was nothing but whiteness ahead of them.

Bonniface gave a cry of joy. "Oh, the wilderness!" he cried clasping his hands as well as he could (for they were plunged deep into his mitts, and big mitts don't work very well when it comes to deeply-felt hand-clasping).

"Dad, are you *sure* you know the way?" asked Edward, rather anxiously.

"It is printed in my heart," said Bonniface, which did not encourage Edward much.

"And Dad," persisted Sophie as they shot onwards, "do remember that, from now on, there'll be holes and hollows hidden by snow."

"Do you think I don't know that?" cried Bonniface scornfully. He pointed ahead of him. "But there are advantages with coming second to someone else."

And, looking more closely, Sophie, Edward and Hotspur saw the marks that been made by Corona's skiddoo shooting ahead of them.

"Where *she* has gone, *we* can go ten times over," cried Bonniface, a little recklessly. "She may have stolen my state-of-the-art skiddoo — but we Sapwoods have the hearts of white Antarctic lions."

"Dad, there aren't any lions in the Antarctic," argued Edward.

"You'll never write a science fiction book if you think like that," his father answered smartly. "You have to *imagine* all sorts of possibilities." And Edward fell silent, thinking this over.

"We'll have to stop soon," said Sophie. "Hotspur needs to have a run-around and maybe a story too."

"Well, evening is coming on," admitted Bonniface. "We will stop then."

Sophie looked up into the clear blue sky. The sun, which had swung from the east to the north, was now edging towards the west, but it was nowhere near setting. It was strange to see a circling sun, rather than a rising and falling one.

"I am making for a snow house I know of," Bonniface explained. "When we were last in the Antarctic, Corona and I, together with a team of explorers (well-trained but not as good as we were) built a snow hut from blocks of ice, and that's where we'll take a break."

"If it's still there," said Edward.

"Of course it'll still be there," cried Bonniface. "Things last forever in the Antarctic. Oh, we'll probably have to dig it out, mind you. But we have plenty of spades on the trailer."

There was no doubt about it, thought Sophie. Her father really *was* an explorer. She was beginning to feel rather tired, but he seemed as buoyant and bright as he had been at the beginning of the endless day. She touched the front of her fleecy jacket where, under layers of clothes, under her polypropylene waistcoat and her thermal underwear, the little pendant hung safely, resting against her, secret and warm. And, as she thought about it, she felt her tiredness disappear. Remembering the pendant had given her new energy.

They drove on and on into the white world, while the sun swung westward. At last they came over a slight slope to see before them, neatly parked beside what seemed to be a small white beehive, the state-of-the-art red skiddoo. A little to the left Corona, armed with a stainless steel shovel, was digging what looked like a ditch around the beehive.

"Oh, Shackleton!" exclaimed Bonniface as if he were swearing. "*She's* remembered that snow hut as well!" And he began muttering with rage as they swooped down the slope towards her.

"Dad!" shouted Edward warningly. "Don't!"

"Don't what?" snarled Bonniface.

"Don't lose your temper," ordered Edward.

"Be kind!" begged Sophie. And though all Hotspur could do was to chirp like a sparrow, you could easily tell he was agreeing with his brother and sister.

"That's *my* snow house!" shouted Bonniface as he drew up beside the red skiddoo. "I built it."

"OK, big shot! But who *helped* you build it?" Corona yelled back, shaking her shovel at him. "And who got here first?"

She looked like a courageous Antarctic warrior princess, but Sophie, squinting at the bits of her face showing between her snow goggles and neck gaiter, thought Corona also looked a little tired. Even warrior princesses can overdo things.

"Don't forget who taught you how to make snow huts," Bonniface was howling. "Me! Me! You'd have been nowhere without me, back then."

"Back then, yes!" said Corona. "But this is now!"

Edward stood up in his skiddoo seat. He was prepared to do a bit of howling himself.

"Come on, you two! Give us a break!" he cried. "Here we are, being brave and bold in the wild, white wilderness. And brave and bold is enough! We don't need to be bad-tempered, too."

Bonniface and Corona stopped shouting at one another. Their two mouths hung open for a moment. They looked at one another, then at the children, then back to one another again.

"Er..." said Corona.

"Well..." said Bonniface.

"You were *quarrelling* with each other," said Sophie. "You're ruining the space and silence by *howling* at one another like a couple of cross wolves."

"You're wasting good energy," Edward went on, "and that means giving off heat which you'll probably need sometime soon. Wasting heat is no way to explore another planet."

"*And* you're wasting time as well," Sophie added. "That icehouse is far too small for all of us. We'll have to build another one."

"Oh, it's big enough for all of us," Corona told her, "but most of it is under the snow. We're going to have to dig it out."

"Then let's get digging," cried Sophie, amazed at her own heroic voice. "Give me a shovel, too!"

"And give me a spade," cried Edward. "It'll be much quicker if we work together."

Corona and Bonniface were still mumbling and staring. Something seemed to be happening under Corona's snow goggles. Yes! No! *Yes*! Slowly, slowly she was smiling. Then she laughed aloud, turning to Bonniface. "What clever kids you've got!" she cried. "And they're right, you know. Fighting like this is insulting the Antarctic. Bonniface... I apologise."

Edward and Sophie could hardly believe it. Bonniface began to smile, too — creakily at first, as if he had forgotten how to twist his mouth upward, glancing across at Corona as if he needed to copy her good smile. But, as it turned out, his own smile spread. It stretched. Corona's laugh took her over — a deep, rowdy, catching laugh that made other people want to laugh as well. Somehow that laugh reminded Sophie of her mother's.

"You're lucky to have such a clever family," Corona said to Bonniface.

"Mind you, there's a great tradition of Antarctic explorers quarrelling with each other," said Bonniface quickly.

"We can do better than those early guys," said Edward, even more quickly.

"Yes! Let's prove we're cleverer than they were," Corona agreed.

And within minutes, there they were – Bonniface, Sophie and Edward, side by side with Corona, all digging in the snow. Even Hotspur was helping, though the spades and shovels were much too big for him. However, he did the best he could, yarring to himself as he did so, like an anxious kingfisher. Every little helps, and Hotspur was determined to do his bit.

At last, Bonniface straightened and stared around. Then he gave such a cry of amazement that the others straightened and stared around, too. They were surrounded by penguins ... tall penguins and short ones... and every single penguin was watching them intently.

"I've never seen anything like this before," said Bonniface.

"Neither have I," said Corona. "Look! Some of those penguins are actually Emperors."

"And some of them are Adelies," said Bonniface, anxious to show that he, also, could name any sort of penguin he happened to be looking at. "Where have they all come from?"

"And why?" asked Corona.

"It's Hotspur!" Edward explained. "He always calls birds around him."

As they watched, the penguins pointed their beaks to the sky and began a noisy penguin conversation, all talking at the same time. Hotspur certainly seemed to be listening to them, his mouth open and his head on one side, frowning a little as if it were hard to follow what they were saying. But then, suddenly, he roared with laughter, rolled backwards in the snow, kicking his mukluks in the air and squawking back at them. Sophie thought that some of the penguins did a sort of penguin-laughing in reply.

"Are they making jokes?" she asked him. But if Hotspur answered at all, he answered her in penguin language, which was not a lot of use to Sophie.

"Fascinating!" cried Corona, deeply impressed. "I've never heard penguins make that sort of sound before. What a remarkable child!"

"Isn't he?" said Bonniface Sapwood, looking at Hotspur with an expression that was half-proud and half-puzzled, as if he truly admired Hotspur but wasn't quite sure just who he was admiring. "His mother loved birds, and somehow he was born knowing bird language."

"Well, we might all have bird language in some ancient part of the brain," said Corona wonderingly, "but most of us don't have any way of making it work for us."

Bonniface had forgotten that she was a bird expert. His expression changed and he quickly began thinking about orders *he* could give.

"OK! Let's all *dig*!" he cried. "We need this house to sleep in. Even though there's no such thing as night at this time of the year, explorers still need to sleep."

"Sleep is vital to explorers!" agreed Corona. "We'll all need some state-of-the-art rest." Sophie could tell she was teasing Bonniface but, just for once, he didn't seem to mind being teased. He gave a silly sort of grin and began digging again.

Down, down, down they dug, slowly uncovering a big, round house built of blocks of ice. And after they had uncovered it they had to find its doorway, then tunnel their way into it, and *then* dig a whole lot longer, emptying it out, for it was entirely filled with snow. The penguins stood around, shuffling and watching, obviously anxious to help Hotspur. If he dropped his spade, penguins waddled forward to pick it up for him. A few of them even took it in turns to peck at the snow. Every little helps.

"I think that'll do," said Bonniface at last, looking proudly at all the work they had done.

"It will," agreed Corona. "Just as well. I'm really tired!"

As for the children, they were all too worn out to answer. Under the tarpaulins on their skiddoo trailers they found their narrow foam mattresses in green plastic covers, waterproof foam pillows and double-down sleeping bags, rolled up tightly

"And now," said Corona, bending over yet another trailer carton, "now for dinner! I'm not only worn out, I'm starving. Let's light the primus and make a big pot of fish soup."

"Are the penguins going to catch fish for us?" asked Edward, but Corona laughed and waved a packet labelled FISH SOUP at him.

It turned out they were so hungry and so tired that they barely noticed the small black plane circling high above them in the cold, blue air of the endless day, the distant whine of its mosquito-like engine often swallowed by the silence of the Antarctic.

CHAPTER 18
Up in the Air

High above, that black plane made wide, swinging circles through cold, blue skies. But inside the plane it was warm and cosy. A butler wheeled a trolley loaded with food though the black velvet curtains that hung across the cabin door. Rancid Swarthy was being served with a delicious dinner – lobster with brandy sauce, a pie stuffed with chicken, onions and sweet red peppers, tossed salad, and a rich dessert called summer pudding.

The Tambo brothers piled their plates so high that food kept falling over the edge. They argued, as they did so, as to which of them deserved the best bits, and poked crossly at one another with the silver forks. Not only that, when they did stop arguing and start eating they were particularly untidy eaters. Crambo sucked in spoonfuls of delicate sauce, making noises like a loo slowly breaking down. Whizzy snuffled as he ate rice with a spoon. Then, hissing through his teeth, he chose a delicious fragment of lobster and flicked it across the cabin at his brother.

It's a terrible thing that a man as cultivated and rich as I am should find himself shut up in a plane with eaters like these two men, thought Rancid Swarthy, dodging a slice of red pepper. Shall I call my bodyguards and have them thrown off the plane?

But then he remembered something. "Horraka-potchkin! They are my bodyguards! If I ordered them to throw themselves off the plane they'd probably refuse to do it, even though I pay them so well. Never mind! They will suffer for this. Once they've exploded Bonniface Sapwood and his family, the Tambo brothers are dead meat."

Glancing up at the luggage rack and a long, black

gun that nestled there, he smiled his Number One smile, but only to himself.

At this moment there actually *was* a sudden explosion, and summer pudding sprayed across the cabin.

"Sorry!" said Crambo, but you could tell he didn't really mean it. Rancid said nothing, but when he wiped the pudding from his face you could see his Number One smile still in place. Whizzy screamed and fainted, but Crambo looked back at Rancid as if he had seen something that interested him. Then he smiled too.

Rancid's mouth dropped open. Crambo's smile was the exact copy of his own. It wasn't quite like seeing himself in a mirror, for his face was long and lean, and his smile had a dip in the middle of it, whereas Crambo's stretched out sideways.

"I *love* that smile of yours," Crambo cried. "Did I get it right?"

"It's *my* smile," said Rancid. "You have to pay me if you want to use it." And the smile quickly vanished from Crambo's face. "Anyhow, our quarry is camping for the night," Rancid added, "and we must return to Scott Base for rest and refuelling."

"Do you mean I'm not getting a chance to blow anyone up?" exclaimed Crambo. He sounded not only disappointed, but a little menacing.

"Tomorrow! Tomorrow!" Rancid promised. "Probably!" he added.

"Of course, we'll blow someone up tomorrow!" said Whizzy faintly, patting his brother's shoulder with a weak but affectionate hand. "You have to humour him," he whispered sideways to Rancid, "or he might get a little – well – *nasty*. He depends on explosions to keep him happy."

Rancid reached for his intercom and gave the pilot instructions to return to Scott Base. Then he slumped back into his chair, but without his usual feeling of self-satisfaction.

People always think a wicked life is an easy one, he thought to himself. They don't realise how difficult it can be. A man has to be really dedicated.

And he refused to look at the brothers from Explosions Ltd. He rather wished he had brought some expert in avalanches instead.

CHAPTER 19

Ghostly Horror

As the Sapwood expedition slept, and Rancid Swarthy headed back towards Scott Base, Captain Cathcardo's ghost paced endlessly up and down, up and down the frozen deck of *The Riddle*. He didn't need sleep. He didn't need summer pudding. Round and round *The Riddle* he went, trying to walk down the gangplank every now and then, but quite unable to do so. He longed to hear his own footsteps just as he used to hear them seventy years earlier — firm and strong, the steps of a true captain. But his feet made no sound at all, and if he tried stamping, his stamping foot would go not only through the ice, but through the deck of *The Riddle* as well. There he would be — stuck, lopsided. Of course, no captain enjoys being lopsided.

So he paced backwards and forwards, lit by his own ghostly light and struggling — always struggling — to remember. He tried to stalk his own memory by going over and over the things he knew already. He was a captain. Yes! He had come to the Antarctic with his old friend, Escher Black, as his First Mate. They had been doing research on meteorites. Yes! Exploring one particularly big meteorite, he had actually found diamonds. A triumph! So what had happened? Why had he become a mere ghost reduced to pacing and puzzling? How had he lost his pendant, and why was he totally unable to leave the frozen *Riddle*? There must be other things he needed to remember first.

As he glided towards the bow of *The Riddle*, he found himself looking, every now and then, out through a little gap hung with long icicles. Beyond the cave which held *The Riddle* there seemed to be a larger, lighter cave — and it also seemed to him that he could make out flickering white shapes on the other side of those icicles. He seemed to hear, as if from a distance, echoing cries, compliments and complaints.

Ghosts! he thought vaguely. There's a cave full of ghosts out there. But I shouldn't be surprised. After all, I am a ghost myself. But who would have thought that being a ghost would be so boring? Now then, Cathcardo! No self-pity! Just remember!

His memory did its best. Meteors, maps and even mukluks rushed one after the other through his ghostly head (which was still slightly crooked, but he would try putting it perfectly straight in a minute). In the meantime, he remembered the way the icy edges of the land had trembled and seemed to shrink into themselves when the meteor struck. The Riddle had been tossed like a toy ship. Why, he'd even written a poem about it all in the ship's logbook.

The ship's logbook!

The Captain came to a standstill. Of course. The ship's logbook! Why hadn't he looked at it before? Soon after he had woken he had seen that logbook sitting safely on the desk in his cabin, but in his confusion he had forgotten it. Suddenly, everything was simple. He'd go down to his cabin, read the logbook by his own blue glow, and every last detail about his fatal voyage would come back to him.

Captain Cathcardo strode to the companionway as

manfully as was possible for a gliding ghost. As he climbed down, darkness fled before him, driven off by his eerie blue light. He stepped through his cabin door as if it didn't exist, for by now he knew that he and the door were real in such totally different ways that they didn't interrupt one another.

There was his bunk. There was his sea trunk. There was his captain's desk. And there on that desk sat the ship's logbook, just as he had seen it when he first woke up, bound and rebound in glassy ice. Soon, he would be breaking that ice and turning the pages. Soon, every detail of the fatal voyage would be his once more.

But things didn't turn out that way, for Captain Cathcardo *couldn't* open his logbook. By now, that logbook, like the cabin door, was real in such a different way from the Captain that his scrabbling fingers went right through the ice, right through the cover, right through the pages. It seemed as if he would never be able find out just what it was he most needed to remember. He stared around in vexation.

And, as he did this, he found himself looking down, accidentally at first, *into* his own bunk and not just *at* it; something he had certainly not done when he had first risen out of it hours, and possibly days, earlier.

It is hard for a ghost to feel terrified. They can be puzzled, irritated and lonely, and, of course, they frighten other people, but they are almost never afraid themselves. Yet now, the Captain (who had been such an adventurous captain all his days – one who had tackled snowstorms and walked on hot meteorites), felt himself melting with terror. His mitts actually began to dissolve in the cabin air. Quickly, quickly, he pulled himself back into shape – for, after all, a ghostly shape was a lot better than no shape at all – staring all the time at the *other* frozen shape tucked into the cabin bunk. It seemed to stare back at him through its shroud of ice. Deep inside that shroud he could make out a twisted face... the face of a dead man... his *own* face.

But that was not what terrified him. He already knew that he must be dead. But through that glacial shroud he could see that the body had a knife plunged into it. Many years ago someone had crept up beside him. Many years ago someone had stabbed him and left him dying in his bunk. The same someone, he was suddenly sure, had been after that box full of diamonds he had brought back after exploring the meteorite. And he knew – knew beyond all doubt – who that someone must have been. For, even though he could not see the knife clearly through the twisting layers of ice, he could see it well enough to recognise it.

There was no doubt about it! *That knife had belonged to his great friend, the First Mate, Escher Black.* And now he also remembered, as if it were yesterday, that Escher Black had been the only one to whom he had mentioned those diamonds. He had confided in Escher Black as if he were telling a happy joke. And during the night his friend must have crept up on him, stabbed him to death and stolen the jewels.

It was all a nasty shock, even for a ghost.

CHAPTER 20

Penguins and Ghosts

Outside, above the snow hut, the sun swung itself in its great summer circle, but Bonniface, his three children and Corona Wottley all slept deeply.

Edward was the first one to wake. He looked at the others stretched on their plastic-covered foam-rubber mattresses, all in double-down sleeping bags of the most colourful and cosy designs. Bonniface had a red sleeping bag, Corona a blue one. Sophie's was a cheerful yellow and Hotspur's was violet. As for Edward's own sleeping bag, it was a bright spring-leaf green.

Feeling a little strange because, after all, he had slept overnight in his two layers of thermal underwear, Edward looked for his clothes. As he slid out of the sleeping bag, a huge, dry cold came at him like a ravenous dragon, so he didn't waste time worrying about washing (and, after all, there wasn't a bath or a shower for miles around). Instead, he scrambled hastily into layer after layer of clothes until he finally reached his survival jacket, his gloves, his mitts and mukluks, and crawled for the door.

He went down three steps and up three steps, almost as if he were tunnelling under the wall rather than simply going through it, and came out into a scene so white and crisp it was like crawling on to the surface of a newly-iced cake. Blue above – and there in the blueness, the bright button of the circling sun! White below, and white all around as far as the eye could see. But as Edward stared, enchanted, he saw that the white was not merely white. In places it sparkled and shone as if it were set with jewels. The slopes of distant mountains shone back at him as if they were acknowledging him to be every bit as wonderful as they were. Some distant ridges were blue-white, others were silver-white, while still others were shaded with a delicate and watery green. Clefts and rifts were grey: not a dull grey, but bright with a soft and shining silver.

And silence arched over them all. There were no voices... no sound of a single skiddoo... no sound of any distant black planes. There were none of the town sounds of distant neighbours, lawn mowers, roadworks, rustling leaves, birds or passing cars. The flag road was behind them. Edward was surrounded by a stillness so ancient he felt he might dissolve into it and become part of it forever. He kept thinking, Now! Now in this next second I'm going *catch* this silence. I'm going to take it in properly! But it always slid away from him. It was too huge to be held inside a simple, human head. It could only be felt in the blood, so in the end Edward gave up trying to listen and just stood there in the middle of it all. Later, he might take notes for his science fiction story. But, right then, all that mattered was seeing and feeling.

"Hi!" said a voice behind him, and there was a bundle of clothes coming out of the ice hut, with Sophie's face looking over the top of the bundle. Edward smiled, but secretly he sighed a little too. He was glad to see Sophie, and yet he had loved the feeling of being alone with the silence. Now he would probably have to talk.

But Sophie didn't say anything for a while, so they stood there, side by side, simply staring, until someone else exploded out of the ice hut behind them.

"Breakfast!" Corona was shouting. "Come on, you kids! I'll show you how to light the little stove." And immediately behind Corona came their father, pushing Hotspur in front of him. Things stopped being beautiful and strange and turned into family life once more, but that was all good fun. Having Corona around was almost like having a cheerful, clever, older sister, teasing but helpful too. Edward and Sophie found that, after all, they were happy to forget mysteries for a while and to concentrate instead on laughing. As for Bonniface – at first he watched them with a kind of smiling surprise, then he began to joke and join in as well, though he seemed a little taken aback to find that the Antarctic might have a funny side to it. Corona poured fuel into two little stoves, and then put water to heat on one of them, and bacon to fry over the other.

While breakfast cooked (and it cooked slowly because a little wind was blowing softly over the ice and bending the blue flames away from under the kettle and pan), Bonniface and Corona sat side by side looking at maps. The old maps showed where (according to the First Mate, Escher Black) *The Riddle* had run into trouble... where the ship (according to Escher Black) had been crushed by ice... and where Captain Cathcardo (according to Escher Black) had tumbled overboard and disappeared. They were still a long way from the place where *The Riddle's* crew (according to Escher Black) had been forced to leave their ship to march overland to safety.

"There was a rumour – a wild rumour – that the expedition brought home diamonds among their geological samples," said Corona a little wistfully.

"I'm not interested in diamonds," cried Bonniface proudly. "I just want to find *The Riddle*, even if it is crushed to kindling wood. Because somewhere among that kindling wood I just might find Captain Cathcardo's logbook. Diamonds! Hah!"

"Oh, yes! Hah!" agreed Corona. "All the same, if we did find a few diamonds lying round I wouldn't leave them behind."

"The ship's logbook is much more important," repeated Bonniface obstinately. "I want to know exactly *where The Riddle* travelled and exactly *what* happened when it got there. I want to walk in Captain Cathcardo's very footsteps."

So saying, Bonniface pointed at a place on his biggest map and started speaking in rather a school-teacherish voice.

"Cathcardo was a hero!" he said. "An Antarctic hero! Mind you, all the crew were brave. But now, before we set out for the day, might be the very moment for me to discuss a strange idea that came to me in my dream." He looked at Corona sternly. "And you're not to laugh at me!"

Corona sucked in her cheeks, making the face of an explorer determined not to laugh at another explorer.

"You see," said Bonniface in a deep, important voice. "I think Escher Black may have been wrong about exactly where they all were when disaster overtook them. He might have misread the maps. I know he *says* that they came all the way round *here*…" his finger moved across the map, "…but perhaps—"

"You're right," burst out Corona, peering at the map and frowning. "That *is* a long way for a shipwrecked crew to have walked. But Escher Black did say—"

"When I had the dream that pushed me into this adventure," Bonniface interrupted, "the dream-thought came to me that Escher Black might have made a *mistake*." He looked challengingly first at

Corona and then at his children, as if they might all want to stick up for Escher Black's story. Suddenly, his challenging expression changed. "Sophie, are you all right?"

"Of course," said Sophie. She did not want to tell him that she had suddenly jumped and clapped her hands across her heart because, under her Antarctic clothes, the pendant had also jumped, just as if it had been given a fright or had recognised an old enemy. "Have you got any idea what sort of mistake Escher Black might have made?" she asked.

"I-I-I thi-i-nk," declared Bonniface slowly, stretching his words to make them sound particularly important, "that we should try to locate the Inlet of Ghosts." He looked around defiantly this time.

"What inlet? What ghosts?" asked Edward.

"Members of *The Riddle's* crew muttered that they had anchored in an inlet flickering with strange, waddling ghosts," explained Bonniface. "Of course, no sensible person believed them, and Escher Black just shrugged and said the crew were all superstitious. (Well, a lot of sailors are very superstitious so he was probably right.) But my research shows that there are other wild tales and rumours about a haunted inlet on this stretch of coast, and it suddenly came to me (in my dream, that is) that we might travel along *here*..."

he pointed at the map "...keeping an eye open for any inlet that other people might not have noticed."

"You're guessing wildly," cried Corona.

Bonniface frowned and sighed. "Yes!" he admitted. "But it is my theory. Are you laughing at me?"

"Most people would laugh at you, but I won't," said Corona. "Because I dreamed that cry of 'Help!' too, you know. And I also felt I'd been given a clue, though my clue seemed to be something to do with penguins."

"Penguins!" exclaimed Bonniface, rather scornfully. "All you can think of is penguins!"

"Hey! Whoa back!" cried Corona. "After all, I listened to your mad theory. You listen to mine. I woke up out of that 'Help' dream, just as you say you did—"

"I did. I did!" said Bonniface quickly. Sophie patted his hand to quieten him.

"—and I woke up (like you) thinking I must go and find The Riddle and rescue whoever it was who was calling for help—" Corona went on.

"That's exactly what I felt," said Bonniface, interrupting her yet again.

"—but I found a little picture haunting a space behind my eyes," Corona said. "White penguins!"

"White penguins!" cried Bonniface. "There are no such things as white penguins!"

111

"Well, that shows how much you know," said Corona sternly. "There are occasional white penguins — albino penguins. I've even seen one or two of them. They have backs and wings of a slightly greyish-white, but their fronts shine like silver. Apart from that they are like any other penguins. They nest and look after their eggs and so on. But there are also wild tales of a whole colony of albino penguins, rather like the tales you were mentioning about the Inlet of Ghosts — and not too far from where you are pointing, either."

Hotspur made a sudden penguin sound. He leaped to his feet and began to dance in the snow as if he were trying to tell them something. But as usual he was trying to tell them about it in some bird language — possibly penguin — so it wasn't much use. Bonniface thought Hotspur might be frightened at the thought of ghostly white penguins and put his arms around him to comfort him.

"Nothing to worry about," he said reassuringly. "Don't be frightened. Even if we do see albino penguins they'll just be ordinary penguins, not monsters or ghosts."

Sophie's mouth fell open.

"But they might be ghosts," she said.

"Sophie, don't frighten Hotspur," said Bonniface sternly, but Edward let out a shout of excitement.

"She's right!" he said. "Dad — you woke up thinking of ghosts and Corona woke up thinking of albino penguins. But suppose, deep down, you were both thinking of the same thing."

"Suppose those crew members who said they'd seen a lot of ghosts had actually seen albino penguins?" cried Sophie.

Hotspur now gave the cry of a triumphant penguin (probably an Adelie, though you couldn't tell if it was albino or not). Corona and Bonniface stared at each other in amazement. At last Corona spoke.

"Let's travel on, keeping an eye open for any mysterious forgotten inlets," she suggested. "And if we do see anything like a ghost or an albino penguin, we'll check it out."

And in the end that is what they did, singing so loudly as they skiddooed along that they failed to hear a tiny throb high in the air above them. Someone was keeping an eye on them once more... and this time it was someone in a black helicopter.

CHAPTER 21

Whoops!

If you think you might need to land on a small patch of Antarctic ice or snow, a helicopter is more practical than a plane, even a ski-plane. But helicopters are much noisier and much more cramped than planes. Of course, Rancid Swarthy had insisted on having a private cabin in *his* helicopter, but he found himself boxed into a space about the same size as a wardrobe and knee to knee with Whizzy Tambo.

As for Crambo Tambo – *he* was sitting with the pilot and had been unnaturally silent for the last hour or so. Rancid wondered if he had fallen out, and rather hoped so. His evil eyes flickered with pleasure at the thought of Crambo crashing helplessly on the frozen coast below. Then he frowned. Just how good was Whizzy when it came to explosions? Crambo had certainly seemed to be the real expert. Rancid gritted his teeth. Even the champagne had lost its fine bouquet.

The edge of the Antarctic was unrolling below them, mostly white, but streaked with black rock and black stony beaches too. When he studied that edge through his state-of-the-art binoculars, Rancid could make out two little spots of colour, bright against the snow. One was red and the other was blue, and they seemed to be fairly frisking along, as if they were quite certain where they were going. Rancid even imagined he could hear the sounds of distant singing and laughing.

"Frisk away! Laugh away!" he muttered, jealous at the thought of other people (and not particularly rich people, either) having a wonderful time. "We'll see who laughs last!"

At this moment, from just beyond the cabin door there came the sound of a crackling *bang* followed by a yell from the pilot. The whole helicopter rocked like an airborne cradle.

"I shall have to take action against that brother of yours," hissed Rancid, dropping his binoculars and slapping the palm of one hand flat against the cabin wall, while he spilled valuable, vintage champagne with the other. "He must be made to understand that a Swarthy Industries helicopter is the wrong place for explosions.

"But he does love a good explosion," said Whizzy, with a sentimental smile. "Give him something to blow up and he's happy as the day is long. And he is getting bored with snow, snow, snow!"

"I don't care whether he is bored or not, he mustn't blow up my helicopter," said Rancid. "And absolutely, utterly not when I am in it. Speak to him!"

"He's just keeping in practice," whined Whizzy. "A explosives man needs to practise all the time. And it's not mere work to him — it's a deeply-felt commitment. Now, tell me more about your early struggles," he added quickly, hoping to distract Rancid from Crambo.

But Rancid was totally sick of both Crambo brothers and was making secret plans to cause them deep suffering. After all, the Antarctic is a place into which people can utterly vanish, so I should take advantage of that, he was thinking, enjoying his own wickedness once more. Captain Cathcardo *vanished*, didn't he? So I'm going to make sure the Crambo brothers vanish too, both of them! Ah, ha, ha, ha, HAH!

His moment of wicked glee, accompanied by a secret Number One smile, passed and Rancid went on plotting...

I'll have to choose exactly the right moment, though. If the Sapwoods do find *The Riddle* and I do manage to get my hands on Captain Cathcardo's lost logbook, I'll need to have the Sapwoods exploded. A good explosion will bury them deeply, and if anyone should record the explosion back at Scott Base they'll think it's just another avalanche. But once the Tambo brothers have brought off a successful explosion they are doomed.

Thinking this, he glanced slyly sideways at the black gun in the luggage net beside him. Then he put down his champagne glass, leaned towards the window and focused his powerful binoculars once more. The red and blue specks swam into sight. He studied the blue one.

"I'll give them something to sing about!" he muttered resentfully. Here he was, the rich and wicked one, forced to share a tiny helicopter cabin with one of the Tambo brothers, while the other was probably tormenting the pilot. "I wish Crambo Tambo was down there, travelling with the Sapwoods. They wouldn't be having a good time then."

And at the exact moment he was thinking this, the coastline below suddenly exploded.

It was as if a bad-tempered volcano had erupted. Snow and ice burst up in a great glittering fountain. Rancid gasped. Vibrations from the blast struck the helicopter which rocked like a rough cradle in the clear Antarctic air. There were shouts and cries from the control cabin and the pilot's voice was plainly heard yelling angrily in some unknown language.

At last the pilot managed to get control of the helicopter. It steadied, and Rancid was able to clap binoculars to his eyes again. On the coast far below he saw white hills that had not been there ten seconds ago. There was no sign of a red skiddoo — no sign of a blue one either. As Rancid stared, stunned and shaken, the door to the helicopter cabin opened. The pilot's voice, sounding even louder now, ran on and on, as both Whizzy and Rancid turned their two accusing gazes on Crambo who was peering in at them with a rare, guilty expression.

"A bomb of mine!" he said. " It just slipped out of my hand. Whoops!"

CHAPTER 22

Smotheration by Snow

"What happened?" screamed Corona. At least, she was trying to scream, but snow was rushing into her mouth and stifling her. Most of her strength was concentrated on spitting it out again. She wiggled her fingers as well as she could, groping for space, but of course her fingers were deep in her mitts and her outstretched arms were firmly held in the grip of a snowdrift.

Only moments ago they had been frisking along the coast, singing and studying the white world around them very carefully, hoping to see some narrow little entrance that every other explorer had overlooked until now. They had all been feeling certain that they – the wonderful Corona-Wottley-Bonniface-Sapwood-and-family exploring team – were about to discover something that no one else had ever noticed before. The lost *Riddle* and its logbook might soon be theirs.

But then the very air around them had roared savagely, as if it were tearing itself in two. Corona had been whisked right off the blue skiddoo and then… well, she wasn't quite sure what had happened next.

"Help!" she tried to shout and, like an echo in her mind, came the cry of her dream. "Help!" Same word! Different voice!

"Breathe," Corona commanded herself, struggling as snow pushed up her nose. With her nose full of snow she had to open her mouth, and of course snow immediately rushed in once more, tingling every tooth in her head and pushing every last little bit of air out of her. I can't believe it, thought Corona incredulously. This is IT. I'm going to die!

But then another mitt flapped against her mitt. Curling fingers inside *that* mitt locked with Corona's fingers in her mitt. (How wonderful fingers are! thought Corona, clinging on desperately.) Someone was dragging… yanking… hauling… tugging. Inch by inch, Corona was being rescued.

She came up out of the snow, with her snow goggles clamped crookedly across the bridge of her nose, rather than her eyes. The hood of her survival jacket hung down heavily behind her, like a huge Santa Claus bag, but filled with snow, not presents. It's nearly Christmas, she thought in a curious dreamy way, wondering about the strange, whooping sound that was filling her ears. What *was* that noise? Where was it coming from? Then she realised that *she* was making the noise as she gasped for air… wonderful air. Gasping was all Corona had time to do.

At last the desperation left her lungs and she was able to begin looking around her, and to ask herself just what had happened to them all. They had been zooming down a rather dangerous ridge, towards a beach covered in thick snow. Corona could remember that clearly. Now the centre of beach, which had been flat and empty, was rounded up into white hills and it was alive with penguins… hundreds of Adelie penguins, and even a few grand and serious Emperor penguins.

Hotspur was in the middle of them, bouncing and bounding and calling out in what was probably a penguin language – but how could you truly tell about penguin language unless you were a penguin yourself? Corona certainly didn't know. And there, beside her, was Sophie – Sophie who had dug with her mitts, then heaved and yanked and tugged, and finally pulled Corona out of the crushing snowdrift that had swallowed her. Sophie was digging yet again. Corona took another long, slow breath, stared up into the sky, and laughed with the relief of being able to do something as simple as breathing. Then she looked at the penguins again.

They were hurrying to cluster around Sophie. They were trying to dig along with her – digging as well as they could with beaks and flippers. It wasn't easy for them, but they did their best. And, as Corona stared, a mitt thrust up through the snow and waved around hopefully. She leaped to her feet. What was she doing, laughing and breathing, when things were still so dangerous for her friends? She must use her newly-won breath to help them.

Corona grabbed the wrist below the mitted hand, while Sophie felt for the fingers. Working together, they heaved and hoisted. A piece of Edward shot out of the snow. An important piece, too! His head. Now, it was Edward's turn to gasp and whoop, though the rest of him was still entirely buried.

"Where's Bonniface? Where's Bonniface?" screamed Corona. "Oh Bonniface! Where are you?"

Edward blinked and whooped and wagged his head from side to side. It is horrifying to realise, just as you are being given the chance to breathe again, that your father might have vanished forever, and that someone you met only yesterday loves your father dearly. Edward stared at Corona, and Sophie would have stared at her too, except that she was far too busy searching the snow for signs of Bonniface – a twitching mukluk, perhaps, or a wiggling finger-tip sticking out of some newly-formed hill. Yet, even as she attempted so desperately to guess where her father might be, Sophie could feel the pendant responding to Corona's cry of fear. It shivered against her skin as if it were just as frightened as Corona.

Then she saw that the penguins had collected around a tumbled stretch of snow and were bowing and pointing with their beaks at a certain spot. Hotspur gave a penguin cry of rejoicing.

"There! There!" cried Sophie, but Corona was already diving into the heart of the penguin circle. This time it was her mitts that plunged down into the snow. This time it was Corona who struggled and strained, who gasped and groaned, tugging gallantly at something no one else could see. Sophie flung her arms around Corona's waist and pulled backwards as hard as she could. Edward's head could do nothing, except shout desperately, "Pull! Pull! Pull!"

By now Corona was flattened down on the snow with Sophie bending over her. Corona's arms were totally invisible, her head was turned to one side and she was struggling and straining with all her might. Then she lifted first her cheek and, a second later, her whole head. Slowly, slowly (helped by Sophie's hauling) she inched upwards, raising her shoulders. Slowly, slowly she struggled back on to her knees, tugging furiously the whole time. But then Hotspur flung his arms round Sophie's waist, dug in his heels and leaned backwards as hard as he could, and somehow, although he was only four years old, the power of his little *extra* weight made an important difference.

Every little helps. Slowly, slowly something was being hoisted into the Antarctic air. Not only that, when Hotspur began to pull, many penguins rushed forward to grab pieces of Corona's survival jacket in their beaks. Leaning backwards they pulled with penguin power, so that, suddenly, almost like a baby being born, Bonniface burst out of that snow, grinning and goggling, but most of all gasping, as the Antarctic, which had been holding him so tightly, gave an icy sigh and surrendered him once more to the world of sky and sea.

Hotspur cried out in penguin language, and all the penguins answered him in chorus. Hotspur danced, and the penguins around him danced as well. "Hooray!" shouted Edward. But Sophie, Corona and Bonniface had no breath for shouting and dancing. They slumped into a pile of soggy explorers, all whooping hard.

Of course, everyone breathes all the time, and nobody thinks about it much, yet it seemed to Sophie that being free to breathe (and seeing her dear family clustered around her all breathing too) was like having the best possible Christmas arrive a day or two early. She would never take breathing for granted again.

"What happened?" asked Bonniface at last, speaking in a weak voice.

"We must have skiddooed into some sort of nowhere place," gasped Corona. "Everything disappeared. Oh, Bonniface!"

"Oh, Corona!" gasped Bonniface. His eyes slid left, then right. "Where's Edward?"

"Where are the skiddoos?" Edward inquired. Sophie looked around and saw that, not too far away, a fresh pile of snow was shivering and jittering as if it were trying to stop something escaping. But Bonniface hadn't noticed that jittering snow. He was too busy staring in horror at Edward.

"My poor boy! He's been beheaded!" he wailed.

"No, no!" cried Corona, leaping to Edward's side. "It's just that we looked for you before digging him out properly."

"I could breathe," Edward pointed out. "You couldn't!"

At which, helped by many penguins, they all went to work excavating Edward. First they loosened him and freed his arms, and then they levered him back to the surface again. The Sapwood family stood there, covered in ice crystals and glittering like people from another planet. They were all very cold and needed hard work to warm themselves up again.

"Did we fall into a hole?" asked Corona. "The ground seemed to vanish under us."

"No! We flew up in the air," declared Edward, brushing crystals of snow from his sleeves and shoulders.

"Flew up in the air? No way! A lot of snow came out of nowhere and tumbled down on top of us," declared Sophie. "Wasn't there a great bang?"

"Did we go up and then down, or down and then up?" asked Corona again. "Everything seemed to happen at the same time as everything else."

"The Antarctic is a mysterious place," said Bonniface, trying to sound as if he were the only one who understood its mysteries. "A volcanic eruption, maybe!"

"We flew up in the air," repeated Edward obstinately. "And while I was turning upside-down I saw the whole coast breaking into pieces."

"It just *seemed* like that," said Bonniface, who didn't want Edward knowing more than he knew. "We must have been caught in some strange Antarctic accident. They do happen," he ended, in his best explorer's voice.

"But what about that black helicopter?" cried Sophie.

Bonniface looked up into the sky and saw the black helicopter was still throbbing and spinning. "Don't bother about stray helicopters," he said impatiently. "What we need is our skiddoos. Begin digging!"

At first they all tunnelled with their mitted hands, beginning at a place to which the penguins seemed to be pointing – a place where the snow was definitely shuddering, and almost at once they found the pointed state-of-the-art nose of Bonniface's red skiddoo, coughing and complaining to itself. Then the penguins screeched and pointed them towards yet another throbbing drift.

Slowly, slowly, slowly, shivering, shaking but working well together (and warming up as they worked) Corona and the Sapwoods excavated the red skiddoo, then searched eagerly under the blue tarpaulin on the back to find their spades. With spades to help them it did not take very long to dig out the blue skiddoo, although it was hidden rather deeper in the snow than the red one had been.

"What *did* happen to us?" Sophie whispered to Edward. It really bothered her that no one seemed to be sure.

"Well, I think that helicopter dropped a bomb on us," said Edward.

Bonniface overhead this. "Edward!" he exclaimed. "This is what happens to a boy who writes science fiction stories. Your ideas get twisted. Bomb indeed! That helicopter up there is a black one, which means it belongs to Swarthy Industries, and they're on *our* side. Remember, they told the Scott Base authorities that we were to have every assistance, which is why we got that state-of-the-art red skiddoo. No more fantasy! Let's pull ourselves together and get on with the next thing. After all, you and I – all of us together – are the heartbeat of a great adventure. A true one, too!"

"Oh, Bonniface," said Corona. " Just as I start to think you are an old-fashioned fuddy-duddy, you say something that makes everything come alive again. You're right! We are the heartbeat of a great adventure. Let's start singing."

"Right!" said Bonniface. "But before the singing begins there's one thing I want to say." He looked at his children proudly. "You kids have been wonderful," he said. "So brave... so capable... it makes me think every explorer should bring his children with him when he sets out on a voyage of discovery. I am proud of you — all three of you!" he declared, patting Hotspur's little hood.

"And we're proud of you, Dad," said Edward quickly. "And if I ever write a good book about an adventure like this, I'll make the hero almost exactly like you."

"Almost?" exclaimed Bonniface, his proud smile vanishing.

"Well, maybe a bit shorter!" said Edward quickly, and Bonniface relaxed, beaming with pleasure once more.

"It takes more than a mere earthquake or volcanic eruption or a possible bomb to discourage Sapwoods and Wottleys," he declared boldly. "Off we go again!"

And so off they went, shooting along the beach,

looking sideways at the huge blocks of ice tossed up by storms and winds, then gazing out beyond the ice to the sea, always smiling its wide, cold, blue smile at them. Meanwhile, on their other side, yet another cliff began to rise, and once again those frozen faces full of icicle teeth began to snarl at them. In spite of possible eruptions and explosions, the Sapwood-Wottley exploring expedition was not defeated. It was on its way.

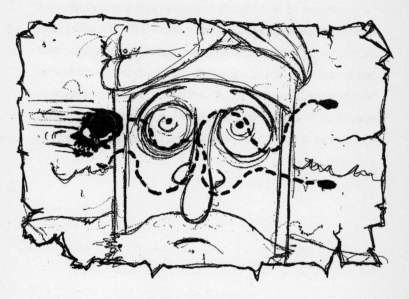

CHAPTER 23

The Captain Waits

The blue line is plaited into the red line, thought the
Captain's ghost, locked in the ice-shroud of *The Riddle*.
They got into some sort of tangle back there, but they
are now they are on the move again. The black skull is
still following them. Is that good? Is that bad? Should
I try to warn them? Of course, I *do* want someone to
bring me the pendant and set me free. But I **don't** want

other people to be trapped in the way I am trapped. Why, I can't even walk down my own gangplank. But even if I did manage to warn them I'm not sure they would take any notice of me. My cries for help may have started them off, but every one of them is coming because they really want to. Whoever they are, they'll be ready to take on their own dangers.

CHAPTER 24

Sophie Believes the Pendant

High, high in the sky above the Sapwoods and Corona Wottley there came the faint beat of a black helicopter, sounding, if you listened to it carefully, like the throb of a wicked heart. But the adult explorers of the Sapwood-Corona Wottley expedition were much too busy steering their skiddoos and showing the Antarctic they were not going to let it shrug them off to notice the sound. Edward and Sophie, however, looked at it suspiciously – Edward because he was still wondering if they had been bombed, and Sophie because the beat of that distant engine was making the pendant shiver against her skin.

Up they went, then down. Out around a wide headland, then in once more... on and on and on. They climbed up yet another treacherous slope and found themselves tilting steeply downwards towards yet another shoreline, obviously covered in deep snow.

"Watch out!" called Edward a little anxiously. But Bonniface was an experience skiddooman. The red skiddoo shot down faster – faster!

"Show off!" shouted Corona, speeding up so that the blue skiddoo went just as fast as the red one, its trailer bouncing about behind it. Edward, Sophie and Hotspur shouted with excitement. Ferocious mouths, full of icicle teeth, snarled at them as they went by.

They shot out grandly on to that long beach which looked so pure and simple, so perfect and untouched that Sophie felt suddenly sorry that they were going to change it all by shooting across it and ploughing it up with the tracks of two skiddoos and their trailers. But, while she was still thinking this, something happened that made her forget the snow, the song and the skiddoos – made her forget everything but the pendant tucked secretly against her skin.

For the pendant began a struggling dance. Even her thermal underwear, her shirts, jerseys and jackets could not stop it from dancing. She could feel it move first right, then left... could feel it twist itself around, then untwist. Sophie felt its dance writing a message, in letters of an unknown alphabet, upon her skin. In one way it tickled, in another it almost hurt, and in yet a third way it filled her with strange happiness for the Antarctic itself seemed to be part of the dance, even though she could see it stretching up, down and out, still and silent, all around her. But mostly the pendant seemed to be trying to tell her something that she needed to be told before it was too late.

"Stop!" screamed Sophie. "Stop!"

"Why?" yelled Edward. After all, what was there to cry out about? Nothing – except (of course) for the sheer fun of things! Yet Sophie's scream had not been a good-fun cry.

"I'll stop once we're over the next ridge," Bonniface shouted back over his shoulder. "We'll have a bit of a breather, and a cup of tea."

"No! Now! Stop now!" Sophie screamed again. "Later will be too late."

"In a minute," Corona promised her, shouting too.

But Sophie unbuckled her seatbelt and sprang to her feet. Then, without a moment's hesitation, she leaped off the trailer of the blue skiddoo, aiming herself as well as she could for what looked like a deep drift of soft snow. The two skiddoos shot onwards for a few yards, almost banging into one another, then stopped untidily. And as Sophie, struggling and flapping like a confused penguin, managed to sit herself up again, she saw her father leaping out of the red skiddoo, racing back towards her, waving his ice axe and wearing an expression she had never seen on his face before – for Bonniface, the bravest of all Antarctic explorers, was frightened. And he was frightened for her.

"Sophie! Sophie!" he was shouting in panic.

"I'm OK," she called, tottering to her feet. Anyone could see she was well and strong even if she was a bit wobbly. So, by the time Bonniface reached her, he had changed from being worried to being angry. The change from frightened to furious took him less than a second.

"How dare you jump out of the skiddoo!" he shouted. "How dare you disobey orders? That's the Antarctic out there. You can't fool around with it."

"What a mad thing to do," said Edward, struggling up behind Bonniface.

"Mad but brave!" added Corona, coming up last of all with Hotspur in her arms.

"Sorry, sorry, sorry!" said Sophie. "But I *had* to. You were going to go right past it."

"Past what?" asked Bonniface, first staring out to sea, then at the snarling mouths in the steep cliff face, and even down a few snarling throats.

"Past the inlet we're looking for. At least, I think so!" said Sophie.

"You *think* so," said Edward indignantly. "*You* think so?" He didn't want Sophie getting ideas before *he* did. Besides, her leap from the skiddoo had terrified him.

Bonniface, Edward and Corona stood side by side, looking at Sophie, looking at each other, then studying the ice face once more. There it was, plain and simple, reflecting snow, sky and sea, and shimmering with blue and silver. Somewhere directly under their mukluks, deep under ice and snow, Sophie thought she could hear the sea gurgling, just as if it were urging her on.

"All right then! Just where *is* this inlet of yours?" asked Bonniface at last, speaking in a particularly sarcastic voice. "Do show me! After all, you've brought us to a standstill... so do *please* show us exactly where, in your official opinion, this inlet we're all longing to find might happen to be. Because,

I confess, I can't see a sign of it." He turned his head from left to right and then back again. "Any inlets? No! Not one! Oh dear! Perhaps my goggles are reflecting the light in a funny way but…"

"Sophie, there isn't an inlet," said Edward.

"There must be," declared Sophie. "There *has* to be. The pendant danced."

"What do you mean, the pendant danced?" asked Corona. "What pendant?"

Sophie hesitated. The pendant was so much her own by now she felt rather shy about pulling it out into the open air. All the same, she scrabbled under several collars, found the bootlace string it hung from, then pulled it over her head and swung it in front of her father.

Bonniface's mouth dropped open!

"Where did you find that?" he asked. "I thought it was lost forever."

"What is it?" asked Corona and Edward in chorus, and Hotspur gave a small squawk like a penguin asking a question.

"I was tidying the big drawer of the upstairs chest," said Sophie to Bonniface. "I found this right at the back of the drawer, and I liked it. I thought it would be all right if I had it. No one had worn it or worried about it for years and years."

"It was one of the first Antarctic things I ever bought," said Bonniface. "I was a boy — a mere child — when I went to my first Antarctic New Year auction. It was just after Christmas, of course, and I had Christmas money. I couldn't afford a sledge or a skiddoo back then, but I picked through a box of oddments and found that pendant." Then he stopped, looking a bit sheepish, and scratched the hood of his survival jacket just as if it had been the top of his head.

"Where did it come from?" asked Corona rather sternly.

"Well, actually, the story was that a member of Cathcardo's crew had brought it back with him," admitted Bonniface looking around him. "That First Mate of his, Escher Black! Or so I was told. But I didn't believe it. People make up all sorts of things when they're trying to sell you something. Anyhow, I bid for it and bought it and then, since it was precious, I hid it somewhere safe, but I forgot where I'd hidden it. Haven't seen it since I was a boy."

"As we came whizzing down the slope this pendant danced," said Sophie. "It went hot and cold, it twisted and turned and spelled out something on my skin. It was really, truly trying to tell me something."

Bonniface looked out to sea once more, then

forwards, along the wide band of snow winding in under them. At last he looked at the cliff again. It snarled at him with its many mouths. He just didn't know what to think, and when Bonniface didn't know what to think he often he lost his temper.

"A dancing pendant doesn't mean anything," he cried. "It *can't* mean anything. And anyone can see — anyone with eyes, that is — there is *no* inlet here."

Saying this he took a mighty swing and struck the ice cliff with his ice axe.

There was a strange tinkling, sharp and fierce, yet somehow musical too. The whole ice cliff shattered like a great mirror. Shards of ice shot out around them, as if the Antarctic were bombarding them with spears. Corona tried to tuck Hotspur under her survival jacket. Flinging his arms over his head, Edward crouched down so that the spears shot harmlessly past him, while Bonniface simply rolled over backwards, pulling Sophie down with him.

Within a second or two things grew still once more. Silence took charge again, tucking quietness in around them. Bonniface, Corona, Edward, Sophie and Hotspur slowly picked themselves up, then stood like tiny, bright statues staring — staring into a sudden star-shaped space that had appeared right in the middle of the ice wall.

It was like looking through a broken window.

Everyone could see that the cliff, for all its angry mouths, had been a mere ice curtain. And there behind it lay a long narrow inlet. A tongue of sea licked upwards from under the ice and lapped softly at the edges of the melting land. The entry to this inlet was so narrow that Sophie could almost have jumped across it, particularly if she had had a trampoline as a launch pad, but beyond the entry the inlet widened out. And on the distant, dimly-lit slopes beyond, they could see strange white shapes waddling and weaving together.

"Ghosts!" exclaimed Bonniface. "It *is* – it must be – the Inlet of Ghosts." But Hotspur pointed at the distant shapes in great excitement, squawked in penguin language and danced a Hotspur dance.

"Not ghosts! Penguins!" declared Corona. "It's that long-lost, legendary colony of albino penguins. It *must* be." Then, she took Hotspur's mitted hands and they danced together – though very carefully, of course. (You have to be careful dancing in mukluks or you strain your upper-leg muscles). Meanwhile, the pendant, back around Sophie's neck, jigged on the end of its string as if it had wanted to join in the fun. And then, at last, all its messages given for the moment, it hung still.

CHAPTER 25

Who Goes Next?

"I never dreamed... " Bonniface began. He looked over at Sophie. "I'm sorry, Sophie," he said in a rare, humble voice. "It just goes to show that, however much a man like me knows, he never quite knows everything."

"That's the most beautiful thing I've ever heard you say," cried Corona, staring through the star-shaped break in the ice cliff. "Oh, Bonniface, shall we... explore?"

"But we'll have to break a bit more ice," cried Edward. "Let's do it!" And he grabbed the ice axe which Bonniface had let fall, and leaped at the cliff as if he were attacking an alien monster on Planet X. Once again the sharp, glassy tinkle of breaking ice mixed into the gurgle and gush of the sea, to make a peculiar Antarctic music. Within minutes, Edward's darting and diving and cracking and crashing had turned the star into a wide doorway through which they could easily stroll.

"Bring torches!" commanded Bonniface quickly. "Got them? Now listen, everybody! This could be dangerous, so watch me carefully." For, though he was in a humble mood, he certainly did not want anyone sliding on ahead of him. (But all Antarctic explorers like to be the first ones to set foot anywhere.)

The inlet, it turned out, was really more of a long dim cave than an inlet. Once inside it, they all pushed up their snow goggles and found themselves wrapped in a silvery twilight. Walls of ice curved up over them but did not quite meet at the top, so that a serpent of sky – a friendly thread of blue – was reflected in a twin serpent of sea.

These blue serpents, the high one and the low

one, kept them twisty company as they wound their way past penguin nests made of black stones. Penguin pairs guarded these nests, and in the distance, lines of white penguins, which did indeed look like parades of ghosts, waddled to the edges where the ice gave up and the sea began. Clustering together, they stared cautiously into the water, shuffling and shifting, until some brave penguin dived in. When this happened, all the other penguins leaned forward, watching anxiously in case a leopard seal or some other penguin-eater should grab the brave one. Then, when they were sure it was safe, the remaining penguins dived and disappeared.

"There must be a way out under the ice and rocks to the open sea," said Corona. "Nesting penguins need to fill themselves with fish. Mind you, it must be restful for these particular birds to be in the shadow of the cave. Albino creatures don't like bright light."

The penguins did not take a great deal of notice of the explorers until Hotspur spoke out. But when he did, every penguin turned its head to stare at him, and those penguins that were not sitting on precious eggs began to waddle along beside the Sapwood party, escorting them through the inlet.

"It's a true Antarctic welcome," said Corona. "Just think! We'd never have found our way in if it hadn't been for Sophie. And look at the respect these penguins feel for Hotspur! Bonniface, you are ten times lucky to have such talented children."

"I know," said Bonniface, "though I didn't realise until this particular morning just how particularly lucky I was." He hesitated, looking around him. "Don't think I'm complaining, and of course it *is* fascinating to have found this place and these penguins, but…"

Corona laughed. "I know what you're going to say," she declared, "because I've been thinking it too. Something's *missing*, isn't it?"

And Corona, Edward and Sophie all cried together, "Where's *The Riddle*?"

Hotspur, however, made a penguin noise, and immediately a whole chorus of penguin noises erupted from beside them, and from the very head of the inlet too. Narrowing his eyes, Bonniface peered into the silvery twilight. There, ahead of them, several penguins seemed to be clustering around something and pointing their beaks at it, though none of the explorers could make out exactly what was being pointed at.

Before anyone could stop him, Hotspur raced away, sliding over the ice towards those pointing penguins, all of whom spread their flippers in welcome, while letting out cries of welcome. It was over in a moment. The pointing penguins stopped pointing and stood back. Hotspur ran past them, and simply disappeared. And, at last, Sophie found she could make out a dark opening low in the wall at the end of the cave.

As the penguins cried out again, she found she could hear — that they could all hear — a chorus of echoes. There must be space on the other side of that opening, and from somewhere inside that space they could hear Hotspur shouting with wonder.

"It'll be safer if I go first," Bonniface said to Corona in rather a begging voice. "Besides, I've been waiting for this moment for years and years. And years!"

"Too late! Look at the kids!" cried Corona.

For Sophie and Edward were already wriggling after Hotspur, leaving the two adults to enjoy yet another argument. Corona looked around. The penguins were all watching them, but she did not care. She laughed, and flinging her arms around Bonniface, gave him a hug and a great big kiss.

"You next, you poor old thing," she said. "I don't care."

"There's plenty of room. Let's go side by side," whispered Bonniface.

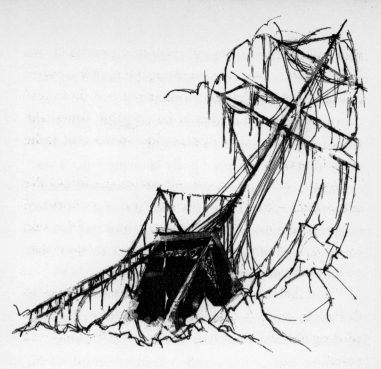

CHAPTER 26

The Riddle at Last

Sophie could hardly believe it. She had slipped out into a cathedral of ice. There was no longer any serpent of sky winding above them or reflecting in the sea below. Indeed, there was no longer any sea. All the same, light was seeping into this cathedral through a maze of chinks and cracks and invisible tunnels in the high roof above them. As she stood there beside Edward and Hotspur they were all transformed from ordinary Antarctic explorers into blue ghosts, trembling with wonder.

And there, before them, was a great, glittering shape... Sophie stared at it frowning, for she found she was recognising it without really knowing what it was. It seemed like something carved by the Antarctic itself – an ice ship, with masts of ice and sails of ice. A railed gangplank, swollen with ice, climbed from cave floor to ship deck, part of the ship and part of the cave, as well.

"It's *The Riddle*," whispered Edward. "It must be."

"*The Riddle!*" agreed Sophie, for as Edward spoke that name, the pendant was growing warm against her skin. It seemed to know it was coming home.

There was a push and a heave behind them, followed almost at once by a heave and a push. Corona and Bonniface slid in side by side, squeezing in as one explorer. As one explorer they leaped to their feet. There was silence again.

Bonniface sighed. "At last! At last! I feel I might shed tears – Antarctic tears."

"Well, don't!" said Sophie. "They'd only freeze on you."

"I know that," said Bonniface a little snappily. He didn't want Sophie giving him good advice. "All right, everyone! Let's go carefully..."

But Hotspur was already climbing, slipping and skidding as he went, and Edward was hurrying after him, holding out his hands protectively in case Hotspur skidded on the treacherous gangplank and toppled on to the ice below

"Hotspur really sounds like an Antarctic boy, doesn't he?" called Sophie, following Edward. "No blackbirds or larks now! He's making penguin noises all the time."

"Oh, Dad! Corona!" cried Edward, stepping on to the deck. "Come up quickly! It's amazing!"

Somewhere behind them in the big cave the penguins set up a great cackling. But the Sapwoods and Corona were all much too filled with *Riddle* astonishment to take any notice. Which (as it happened) was rather a pity. The penguins were trying to warn them of something.

CHAPTER 27

Villains Can't Trust Other Villains

The black helicopter came thumping down on the beach in front of the Inlet of Ghosts, now easily seen behind the great break in the ice wall. The Tambo brothers and Rancid Swarthy stared into the silver twilight trying to make out the end of the inlet. They could see the blue serpents of sky and sea, one above and one below. They could see the white shapes of the ghostly penguins who immediately set up a great chorus of alarm.

"What's in there?" Whizzy asked, being careful not to look too closely at Rancid. He was trying not to notice the gun that Rancid was now carrying with him.

"Something that needs to be exploded," suggested Crambo eagerly, and he looked at Rancid hopefully. Crambo was not impressed with the gun – not in the least.

"No exploding," said Rancid quickly. "At least, not until I say so. Now, listen carefully. I shall follow Bonniface Sapwood in there and check things out. Don't do anything noisy or rash or you won't get paid. Just enjoy a nice, restful five minutes, drinking in the beauties of the Antarctic. I won't be long. And when I come out again, you can have a real treat, because I will almost certainly want a dramatic explosion."

A blissful expression settled over Crambo's face.

"You do realise it will take more than one explosion to close this cave off, don't you?" he said. "I'll arrange for two or three of them."

"Good man!" said Rancid heartily, looking at Crambo with approval for the first time in that long Antarctic day. "But promise me faithfully you won't set off any explosions until I tell you to."

"I promise! I promise!" cried Crambo, though his eyes shifted in a most untrustworthy fashion.

Rancid gave his Number Two smile, causing Whizzy to gasp and shrink away.

"I'll keep an eye on him, Sir," he promised in a shivery voice.

"I am sure you will," sighed Rancid Swarthy, "because, after all, if you should forget... if you should be even slightly careless... you won't get paid, will you? And I know you dearly love money."

"Oh, we do, Sir," cried Whizzy and Crambo as one.

"Never forget how wonderful it is to be paid," said Rancid. "Live in hope!"

Then he turned and set off into the cave, a sinister figure in his black survival jacket and black mukluks, not to mention the long, black gun balanced across his bent, black arm.

The Tambo brothers stared after him. "Crambo," said Whizzy after a moment, "do you think we should trust Mr Swarthy? I mean, in view of what he was carrying under his arm?"

"You mean that gun of his?" asked Crambo, blinking thoughtfully. "Yeah, you're right. Makes you think a bit, doesn't it?"

Whizzy reached up and patted Crambo's cheek

with his mitt. "Keep on thinking, you clever boy," he said, smiling and nodding.

"Of course, he might be going to blast a few penguins," suggested Crambo, "but I think there might be a bit more to it than that."

"So do I," said Whizzy. "And the thing is, if he shoots the explorers and then we blow up this cave so that it vanishes from all human knowledge, well then we're witnesses, aren't we? Can we be sure he won't..." Whizzy paused.

"...shoot us!" finished Crambo. They looked at each other.

"He just might," said Whizzy at last, "so I think we ought to start off by booby-trapping the helicopter. Then, if he so much as points that gun in our general direction, we'll explain to him that if we don't get home safely, the helicopter will explode and he'll be stuck out here in the icy wastes. He's bound to take that seriously. I know I would."

"Me too!" agreed Crambo. "I'll do the helicopter first. That way we can be sure of Rancid Swarthy. And if the pilot asks us what we're doing, we'll say we're cleaning it up for him."

"Good idea!" said Whizzy. "Just booby-trap it in ways that only we know about. Aha! Nobody's going to put one over on Explosions Ltd. Let's go!"

"It'll be a complicated job," agreed Crambo, his face bright with pleasure. "I'll begin at once."

And so he did.

CHAPTER 28

The Logbook at Last

How strange it was to be on an old ship that had been frozen in ice for seventy years! Ever since they could remember, Edward, Sophie and Hotspur had heard the name *The Riddle*, THE RIDDLE, murmuring around their house... Echoes lurking in odd kitchen corners had whispered "*The Riddle*" to them.

Whenever they opened their toy cupboard, the

name *"The Riddle"* had hissed from corner to corner. For after their mother died, whenever Bonniface had trouble sleeping, he would pace from room to room in the early hours of the morning saying the name of that lost ship aloud. *"The Riddle! The Riddle! The Riddle!"* he had exclaimed. *"The Riddle?"* he had asked himself, partly because it was the name of the lost ship and partly because life puzzled him so much. But though the echoes of his bewilderment had haunted the house, there had never been an answer.

And at last they were actually on *The Riddle* itself. Even though they were all wrapped in thermal underwear, in coats and three layers of trousers, in woolly hoods, inner gloves, outer gloves, mitts and mukluks. Even though they were not actually touching the true wood of *The Riddle*, sheathed as it was in ice, they could feel the ship was almost alive, under their mitts and mukluks.

"Escher Black was certain it had been crushed to kindling," murmured Bonniface, looking around him.

"We mustn't take any notice of anything Escher Black said," replied Corona. "I've always thought it was very suspicious – I mean, the way he came home from the Antarctic and grew rich all of a sudden. Now! What do we look for next?"

Bonniface was in no doubt. "We must find

Captain Cathcardo's logbook," he cried. "Whatever happened *here* will be written down *there*."

"We might even find a treasure map!" said Corona. "Captain Cathcardo will have written down exactly what happened in the last days. There might even be some diamond clues."

"Oh, yes!" said Bonniface, but carelessly as if diamonds weren't worth thinking about. "The main thing is he will have written down his thoughts and observations in that logbook. If we find that, melt it very carefully and read it, we will understand just what happened at last."

And off went Bonniface, once more determined to go first, which was probably a good thing, for finding a way through *The Riddle* was a little like finding ones way through a refrigerator which has been filled with a thousand leftovers and then totally neglected for years and years. They all turned on their torches, and the torchlight picked out strange shapes and openings. It was all confusing, for everything looked like something else and most explorers would have been utterly confounded. But Bonniface had studied the plans of *The Riddle* since he was Edward's age – since he was Hotspur's age. Ice or not, he knew that whole ship by heart.

"The companionway is over here!" he called, and led them without the slightest hesitation. At the sound of his voice – so happy, so sure of itself – the pendant throbbed against Sophie's chest like a little, extra heart.

"The strange thing is," said Sophie to Edward and Corona, "this ship has been empty for years and years, but it doesn't – well – it doesn't *feel* empty, does it?"

Corona and Edward stopped and stared around uneasily.

"I know what you mean, but it *is* empty," said Edward. "It must be."

"Perhaps there are penguins hiding in corners," suggested Corona.

"Come on!" called Bonniface impatiently from a little way ahead.

They moved off after him.

"It can't be penguins," muttered Sophie, "because Hotspur always calls out to penguins and they come when he calls. It's something else."

"The penguins back there in the big cave are certainly making a row," said Corona half-turning her head. "Anyone would think they were trying to warn us about something."

"Faster! Can't you go faster?" cried Bonniface impatiently. "Ah! We go down here."

So down they all went, following Bonniface down the companionway which was so iced-up they had to kick ice away to make room for their mukluks. And slowly but surely they did find a way – first Bonniface, with Hotspur clinging to his back, then Edward, and then Corona, who every now and then helped Sophie, who came last of all. She still had the strangest feeling that someone was watching them – that someone had been watching them from the very first moment they had slipped in from the outside cave – that someone had watched them slithering and swaying up the gang plank, and was still there, listening to everything they had to say. This strange someone was not in any particular corner or cabin, but somehow all over the ship... it was someone who could be up or down, here or there, at one and the same time.

"At last! The captain's cabin!" cried Bonniface, flashing his torch up and down, then touching a surface that looked like thick, cloudy glass. But if you peered into that glass, it was possible to make out solid, old oak somewhere in the heart of it.

Bonniface tried to open the door. It would not open. He leaned against it. It still would not open. He pushed his shoulder against it... .

"Let me help!" said Corona, and they pushed together. The door stayed shut.

They pushed and heaved. Bonniface, now filled

with violent enthusiasm, made every one stand back while he flung himself against that door, over and over again. But he bounced off uselessly, probably bruising himself in spite of all his layers of padded clothes. Then Edward and Sophie put down their torches and joined in. All four of them pushed and heaved and bounced together. But the door still refused to open.

Then Hotspur moved towards the door, looking a little scared because, what with the thrusting, heaving, pushing and bouncing, it did seem he might be squashed or trodden on.

"Get that boy out of here!" yelled Bonniface, who wasn't so much afraid of treading on Hotspur, as on Hotspur spoiling the rhythm of the heaving and bouncing. However, Hotspur was too quick for him and, before anyone could stop him, he joined in. Every little helps! Hotspur's four-year-old heaving and bouncing might not have been much in itself, but it made a difference. Even in the darkness, Edward could see a web of silver cracks running through the ice as it splintered away. At last, at last, the door inched open.

Squeezing into the captain's cabin was like trying to cram into an icebox. Bonniface's torchlight fell on the foot of a bunk bed, then swept on to a desk. And there on the desk was what looked like a thick parcel of ice. It had been there for many years, and each year the Antarctic had wrapped it around with yet another layer of ice. Bonniface took a breath… bent over it… shone the torch on it… peered into it. He could just make out letters swimming like distant golden fish in deep water! They wavered and twisted, but Bonniface stared so sharply, so narrowly, they could not confuse him. LOGBOOK, said the golden words.

"I've found it!" he cried, and, in spite of the danger, tears really did stand out in his eyes.

"Don't cry! Don't cry! You'll freeze!" shouted Corona, and she was right. Bonniface's top eyelashes froze to the bottom ones. He could not even wink or blink!

"Turn the torch on his face," cried Sophie, and fortunately Corona took this good advice. It was a powerful torch and the light it gave off was enough to melt Bonniface's frozen tears so that she was able to mop them away quickly.

"We'll take it back to Scott Base, melt the ice and read it," said Edward, staring at his father standing there with The Riddle logbook in his hand and remembering how The Riddle and its many mysteries had haunted them for as long as he could remember.

"I'm holding it!" cried Bonniface. "Holding Captain Cathcardo's logbook at last. And I owe it to all

161

of us – to Corona and…" he looked at his children in the dark cabin "…to my kids. Even Hotspur!"

The moment was so exciting, the cold was so ferocious, that none of them had noticed that the ship beyond them was full of noises… full of cracking and grumbling. Then, suddenly, everything around them transformed. The light of a torch far more powerful than their own torches fell on them, while the open doorway of the cabin darkened… and not because the door had closed.

"Ah! Good evening, all!" said a new voice, a horrid voice, "if it can be said to be evening when, somewhere outside, the sun is still high in the sky."

They all spun around. Though they were blinded by that torchlight, they knew someone was staring in at them – someone in a black survival jacket, with a black hood above and black mukluks below. This darkly-dressed man was even darker than the still air of the frozen *Riddle*. And the gun he was pointing at them was black too.

Sophie immediately felt she somehow knew this man, though, at the same time, she was also perfectly certain that she had never seen him before. What she did know for sure was that, under her clothes, the pendant suddenly grew colder and colder. It was recognising something about their new enemy, who flourished the gun in one hand and pushed up his snow goggles with the other.

"Rancid Swarthy!" cried Bonniface and Corona together. It was a name Sophie had sometimes heard on television and she vaguely remembered seeing that wicked face in the papers and magazines.

"It is always gratifying to be recognised," the man said. "I advise you not to argue with me, Bonniface Sapwood, or I might try and shoot you. And I am not a good shot. Why, I could even hit one of your children. Now, give me that logbook."

"But I don't understand," said Bonniface. "What are you doing here?"

"Looking for the logbook!" said Rancid Swarthy. "What else?"

"But I'm planning to bring it back to you — well, bring it to our local museum," said Bonniface. "It needs to be lovingly restored. Then you'll be able to read it there. Everyone will."

"That diary must not be opened by anyone but me," said Rancid Swarthy. "You see, somewhere during his long-ago travels, the late Captain Cathcardo explored a fallen meteorite. And on the surface of that meteorite I believe he found diamonds."

"Oh, yes! There was some tall story about Escher Black bringing a few diamonds back with him," said

163

Bonniface with a cheerful laugh. "It's just old gossip, though. And anyway, finding an outer-space meteorite would be even more amazing than finding a few diamonds."

"Diamonds are best," said Rancid in the voice of a man entirely sure he is speaking the truth. "Absolutely the best! The thing is, Captain Cathcardo may have hinted somewhere in the logbook you're holding just where that meteorite fell. The logbook must be mine."

"Of course it belongs to you," cried Bonniface. "To you – to me – to everyone! Knowledge belongs to the world."

"I was frightened you might say something like that," said Rancid. "You see, when I said it belonged to me... I meant it belonged only to me."

Bonniface stared at him. "You can't mean it," he cried.

"But I do," Rancid assured him. "I'm generally not a sincere man, but on this occasion I am utterly, entirely sincere. I am going to take the logbook. I am going to shoot you all in this very cabin. Then I am going to leave this miserable ship in this miserable cave. And my minions are going to blow up the cave. At this very moment the firm of Explosions Ltd are hard at work arranging a great detonation. As I climb into my helicopter, they will set it off… the cave will collapse… your bodies will be buried here in the ice, along with *The Riddle* and those wretched white penguins, and I will sweep off, logbook and all, in my black helicopter."

"You can't do that," cried Corona in horror. "Those penguins out there are rare birds."

Rancid laughed scornfully. "Penguins! Ha ha ha ha! Who cares about a lot of penguins? I will take that logbook and defrost it. I will read it at my leisure and, sometime later (this time next year, say, when you and your family and your silly expeditions will be almost forgotten), I'll set up a small expedition of my own, locate the very place where Captain Cathcardo discovered those diamonds, dig down to the meteorite, and mine a whole lot more. I will be rich! Rich! Rich!"

"But you're rich enough already," cried Corona.

"I *am* rich," agreed Rancid. "but not rich enough. It isn't possible to be rich enough."

As he said this, Sophie, listening in horror, became aware of something very peculiar happening just beyond Rancid Swarthy. Smoke began rising and twisting just over his left shoulder. And it seemed this smoke was trying to take on a definite shape… trying to *be* something or someone.

"Now, pass me that logbook and I will see to it you die quickly," Rancid said. "You won't feel a thing. But if you hesitate, it will the worse for all of you. Even the littlest one will feel the power of my anger."

The smoke was forming a face... a face with a curious, blue shine to it. Once again Sophie felt she already knew that face well. She shot a sideways glance at Edward. He was certainly looking at Rancid... but she could not tell if his horrified expression was because of the gun, or the twisting blue face. Hotspur, however, piped and pointed.

"Tell that ridiculous child to shut up," hissed Rancid.

"But — but — there's someone behind you," stammered Sophie. "Someone blue!"

"My dear, there is no way I'm going to fall for an old trick like that," said Rancid. "You think I will snatch a glance over my shoulder and that you will have a chance to dash the gun from my hand. But I am not to be taken in by such tricks. Give me that logbook immediately!"

With every passing second the face was becoming more and more visible... and by now Sophie knew exactly who it was. So did Bonniface and Corona, but being grown up they couldn't believe in it as easily as Sophie, Edward and Hotspur could.

"It can't be… " Bonniface began.

"*Oh, but it is!*" cried the face at Rancid's shoulder.

It sounded like a huge echo. It sounded like wind blowing down one of the Dry Valleys. At the same time it sounded like something never heard by human ears. It was not shouting – it was not even particularly loud – yet somehow it filled every little space in the whole of *The Riddle*. It rang off icy surfaces, seen and unseen. It echoed in the cabin and up the companionway, and then came back at them from all directions.

Rancid gave a convulsive leap and, even though there was so little space to spin in, he managed to spin around in the cabin doorway. The blue face smiled at him – a smile much more terrible than anything he could smile himself. It seemed to be melting. Then it pulled itself together again.

"Oh, it's my old friend and murderer, Escher Black!" said the voice, and the name rang through *The Riddle*. "*Escher Black! Black! Black!*"

"Captain Cathcardo!" screamed Rancid.

"*You traitor!*" said the face. "*You killed me. You stole my crew! You stole my diamonds!*"

"It wasn't me!" screamed Rancid. "Escher Black was my grandfather. I never got on with him. It wasn't my fault. I'm not in the least like Escher Black. I was pretending just now. I'm really very nice."

"You look just like Escher Black!" said Captain Cathcardo. "But that doesn't matter. You think like Escher Black, and that *does* matter."

Rancid fired his gun. He fired it over and over again, yelling all the time.

"I'm not Escher Black." (*BANG!*) "I'm much, much cleverer than Escher Black!" (*BANG!*) "He was a mere thief! An uneducated thief!" (*BANG!*) "I am an executive!" (*BANG!*) "I rule a business empire." (*BANG!*) "Kings and presidents ring me up and send me birthday cards." (*BANG!*)

But none of the shots made any difference to the ghost of Captain Cathcardo and, at last, Rancid had to let the useless gun drop to his side. Quick as a wink, Edward leaped in to snatch it from Rancid Swarthy's clumsy mitts.

"Catch!" he shouted, tossing it to Bonniface. But Bonniface's fingers were locked around the logbook. He would not — he *could* not let it go! He was frozen to it.

It was Corona who pulled the gun out of the air. As for Rancid Swarthy, he had barely noticed his gun being snatched away. He was far too busy flinging himself at the ghost, pummelling it with his black-gloved hands.

The ghost moved, but not to protect itself. Indeed, it stepped forward and flung out its arms to hug

Rancid. There was a curious convulsion in the cabin doorway. Just for a moment it was hard to tell where Rancid left off and the ghost began, for they seemed to have melted into each other and become the same single person. Sophie thought it was as if Rancid was struggling and shouting somewhere inside a misty blueish envelope.

And then the ghost slowly took its own form once more. Somehow, it flowed out around Rancid, and not merely around him either, but right *through* him. Rancid gasped… struggled… crumpled and fell to his knees, giving strange whooping cries almost as if his throat and lungs had been filled with snow. The ghost moved away from him, leaving him twisting on the floor. It stood beside the frozen bunk and looked at Bonniface, still clasping the diary. Then it looked towards Corona, who was holding the gun as if she was not quite sure what to do with it. After that, the ghost looked into Sophie's eyes.

"I can tell you're brave," it said. "See that bunk there? Lift the blanket. It's frozen, but see if you can lift it all the same."

Sophie and Edward struggled to shift that frozen blanket. They pushed and pulled until it cracked and came to pieces in their mitted hands Under that shattered blanket lay a figure, its open eyes peering up at them through a shroud of ice. Its face was shrunken and withered, but there was no doubt that they were looking at the body of Captain Cathcardo himself. Rancid Swarthy yelled and writhed in the doorway, but nobody took any notice of him.

"Escher Black killed me," Captain Cathcardo said. "I thought he was my friend. I was so excited, I told him about the meteorite and showed him the diamonds. So he stabbed me with his knife, and stole the diamonds. I think he even wrenched my good-luck pendant from around my neck. I seem to remember him waving it in front of my dying eyes, laughing as he did so. I don't know for sure what happened after that. I suppose he sailed the ship into this outlet, told the crew some story and led them away. You may be able to tell me the end of my own story. And I do hope that, now you are here, I might be set free at last... free to go on to the next thing."

"Help! Help!" screamed Rancid. "What's happened? Where has the world gone?"

"It's still around you," Sophie assured him.

"No, it isn't!" he yelled back. "The world's gone. Gone! Where did all this blue mist come from?"

"Why haven't you gone on to the next thing before this?" Edward asked Captain Cathcardo. "I once read that ghosts couldn't cross running water, but nearly all the water here is frozen."

"I think I needed my pendant. It was virtually part of me," the ghost explained. "And perhaps I needed to haunt my logbook." It smiled at Bonniface. "Now I know that the right person has found it I might be free to go."

"Take me with you!" screamed Rancid, who was still gasping and whooping and wailing and waving wildly on the floor behind them. "I'll scrape off some of the diamonds from my bedroom ceiling and give them to you. I promise I will."

"I don't need diamonds..." began Bonniface. "I want to know!" He looked at Captain Cathcardo again. "I just want to *know!*"

"I understand," said the ghost. "I was like that too, once upon a time."

"Will you really be able to go on to the next thing?" Sophie asked curiously. "What *is* the next thing?"

"That's what I'm hoping to find out," the Captain replied.

Sophie unzipped her first jacket so that she could pull her scarf free. She unwrapped her scarf so she could get at her first collar.

"Sophie!" cried Corona. "Don't! You'll freeze."

171

But Sophie had already unzipped her second layer, and was feeling quickly under her third fourth and fifth layers. She ducked her head as she lifted the cord of the pendant over her head.

"Is this yours?" she asked.

Captain Cathcardo gave a cry of happiness. "It IS mine!" he cried. He took it from her. "It was stolen from me, but it is mine. See? I can't hold anything else, but I can hold this."

The pendant swung safely from his gloved fingers.

Corona, in a particularly motherly way, was hastening to wrap Sophie's scarf back around her throat, to pull up her neck gaiter, to zip up her second layer, and then to zip up her first. Meanwhile, Rancid had somehow staggered to his feet.

"Help me!" he was shouting as he toppled to the right, toppled to the left and then fell over again. His black mukluks kicked at the air. "Why am I going in all directions at once?" he screamed.

"Let's climb out on to the deck," suggested Captain Cathcardo.

"I thought you were going on to the next thing," said Edward.

"Another five minutes won't hurt me," said Captain Cathcardo, moving towards the door. Rancid howled with apprehension and rightly so, for the ghost walked through him for the second time. "I fancy one last look at the ice," said the Captain, making for the companionway.

They all followed him, stepping past Rancid — Bonniface hugging the diary, Corona hoisting Hotspur on to one shoulder and carrying the gun over the other, Edward scooping up Rancid's powerful torch as he wriggled by, and Sophie (who came last of all) managing to jump right across him, cleverly avoiding his frantic kicking.

"We'll come back and get you," she promised (because, after all, you have to be kind even to someone nasty or it means you are being nasty yourself). "Try to relax!"

"Wait for me! Wait!" howled Rancid, so desperate by now that he actually did manage to come tumbling after them, crashing against first one frozen wall and then against the other. Sophie couldn't help feeling sorry for him in spite of his wickedness. Desperately, he climbed up after them, crashing and tumbling over the deck. And then, as the Sapwoods and Corona slipped and slid down the gangplank, grasping the rail all the way, Rancid somersaulted over that rail, crashing on to the ice below. "Help me!" he howled yet again.

"We can't just leave him," said Sophie reluctantly, and when they stood on level ground once more

Bonniface helped his flapping, flopping enemy to his feet.

"Lean on me!" he suggested, and Rancid did lean on him which was very uncomfortable.

Light seemed to flare up around them. It was a dim light, but to anyone emerging from the depths of *The Riddle* it was almost dazzling. They all squeezed back through the little gap connecting the two caves to see, once again, those blue serpents of sea and sky and the ghostly white penguins. In the distance, through the big hole that Bonniface and Edward had broken in the ice wall not so very long ago, they could see sunlight. And, black against that brightness, stood an unexpected figure. Someone, it seemed, was waiting there, peering in at them anxiously. Beyond this figure they could also make out part of a black helicopter.

"Take me home!" howled Rancid. "Take me home!" And, letting go of Bonniface's shoulder, he stumbled ahead of them towards the helicopter.

"Let's be careful!" Corona hissed sideways to Bonniface. "Remember that smile! He's treacherous — through and through. He might have guns on that helicopter."

"You don't have to worry," said the ghost. "I altered all that as I went through him. I didn't know I could do such things, but I found I could. I mean, he's doing his best to be treacherous right now, but his wickedness will never work again. It must be very upsetting for him. Anyone can see how he depends on it."

As they watched, Rancid sprang in his lopsided way towards the mouth of the cave, and the man waiting there rushed to meet him. But Rancid sent him sprawling and blundered past, making for the waiting helicopter. The sprawling man, a short, weedy little fellow, picked himself up and ran frantically after him.

"No! Wait, Sir! Wait!" he was howling. "Just hang on a bit! Crambo's still on board." He tripped over but leaped to his feet once more, shouting all the time. "Crambo hasn't finished the... that is to say we can't blow up the cave just yet! Sir, we can't take off. There's no pilot on board."

"I'll fly it myself," Rancid shrieked over his shoulder. "I've had lessons."

Climbing the helicopter steps, he dived through its door and vanished from sight.

"Wait, Sir!" the short man cried over and over again, bounding wildly after Rancid. "You don't know what Crambo's been up to." The helicopter was already throbbing and shaking. The short man leaped up the steps and vanished too. Then the steps fell backwards on to the snow, and the helicopter lifted into the blue and gold of the endless day of the Antarctic summer. They watched it grow smaller and smaller as it wobbled wildly off into the north.

The Sapwoods, Corona and the ghost wound their way through flocks of white penguins, taking care not to stand on any nests. As they came to the mouth of the cave they were astonished to find a stranger sitting on a rock and staring out after the helicopter with a stunned expression.

"They've left me behind," he said. "I can't work out what's going on. Me, I'm from Scott Base. I was told to pilot the Swarthy Industries helicopter for Rancid Swarthy, which I did. I landed exactly where Mr Swarthy wanted me to land – just over there. Then, after Mr Swarthy had shot off into that cave, one of the passengers – the big man – Crambo, they called him – ordered me off the helicopter. I don't know what he was up to, but I suspect it might be something to do with explosions. He was certainly one of those blokes who liked things to go with a bang. And, hey – that little joker didn't want anyone trying to take off in the helicopter, did he?"

"No," agreed Corona. "He didn't. But he jumped into it himself, for all that."

176

"I think he wanted to stop his brother doing whatever it was he was doing," said the pilot. "And before they really knew what was going on, they were up in the air."

"Gone!" said Bonniface, sighing with relief. "I'm glad they've gone." But as he spoke there came the sound of a distant explosion, and a sudden fierce burst of light flared up beyond the headland.

"Doesn't sound good," said the pilot. "I don't think we'll hear from them for a while."

"We'd better try to rescue them," said Edward doubtfully.

"They wouldn't come to your rescue," said the pilot, shaking his head.

"But we're *better* than they are," exclaimed Sophie. "We have to be."

"Where's my cell phone?" cried Bonniface a little wearily. "I'll call in the experts."

By now they were all standing out in the Antarctic summer light, with many albino penguins, blinking in the sunshine, standing around them. Although it was hard to feel properly worried about anyone as wicked as Rancid Swarthy, or even Explosions Ltd, Bonniface began searching the trailer of the blue skiddoo for his cell phone so that he could ring Scott Base and arrange for a Rancid Swarthy search party.

But the ghost showed no anxiety. "I had forgotten how beautiful it was," he said, staring around him.

The children and Corona Wottley did not even glance at him as he said this because they were too busy looking outward themselves — out across snow, and ice and sea to an ethereal line of peaks and glaciers. They couldn't help feeling happy... happy simply to be alive.

"Maybe it's better than being on another planet," said Edward.

And suddenly an entirely new voice chimed in — a voice that no one had ever heard clearly before.

"Wonderful world!" it said.

"Hotspur!" screamed Sophie. "Hotspur said something!"

"Wonderful!" repeated Hotspur, beaming around at everyone, thrilled by his own cleverness.

The strange thing was that, right then, having Hotspur speak actual words suddenly became the most exciting thing that had happened all day. It was only when they had stopped fussing over Hotspur, praising him and trying to get him to say a whole lot of other things, that they looked up at each other, all smiling, and saw Captain Cathcardo was dissolving into the air. It was a little like watching grains of sugar melted by hot water, except that he was being melted by light.

The ghostly figure smiled back at them as he slowly disappeared. He waved at them; his lips moved. There was no sound but they could tell he was saying, *goodbye*... *goodbye*... *goodbye* to them all, *goodbye* to *The Riddle*, *goodbye* to the wild, white world of the Antarctic. Set free at last, he was going on to the next thing...

CHAPTER 29

Antarctic Wishes

"Let's go on," said Edward. "Let's go all the way to the South Pole."

"I know just how you feel," said his father and Corona together.

"But we can't," added Corona. "We've got just enough fuel to take us home and a little bit over in case of accidents. And don't forget we've now got an extra passenger as well."

"Thanks," said the pilot, looking deeply grateful.

"Besides," added Bonniface, "this has been the easy part. Going to the South Pole would be ten times as hard. We'll do that some other time. In any case," he added, "I can't wait to tell everyone that I've found the lost *Riddle*."

"*Who* found it?" asked Corona giving him a hard look.

"I mean '*we*'," cried Bonniface quickly "*We* found it. You, me and the kids! Oh, Corona, we'll be famous all over again. Aren't you glad to be able to have such adventures?"

"I wasn't too sure half an hour ago, but I am right now," said Sophie.

"I'm still thinking about it," said Edward.

So they collected themselves, trekked over to the skiddoos, repacked themselves and rearranged themselves. Then they got off the skiddoos, unpacked themselves and rearranged themselves some more until, at last, they had fitted everyone and everything on in a comfortable way. Then off they went, shooting around the coast once more.

"If people come to look at *The Riddle* I do hope they're kind to the albino penguins," said Sophie to Corona. "I don't think those penguins will like big crowds."

"They'll have to arrange it very carefully," said Corona. "They'll have to wait until the nesting season is over, for example. And perhaps they might even haul *The Riddle* back round the coast and set up a *Riddle* museum at Scott Base. Then the penguins would have the caves all to themselves again."

"We'll see," cried Hotspur, already sounding as if he knew everything. But sometimes little kids are like that.

So they skiddooed back past the place where they had been buried in snow, then back to the ice hut where they rested, ate dinner and wrote in their diaries, and slept and dreamed while the sun edged on around them. Then they woke up, ate breakfast and set off again.

"You know there's something important I'm forgetting," said Corona fretfully. "I can feel it flicking around in my head, but I can't quite catch hold of it."

"It's funny you should say that," Bonniface said, "because there's something I've forgotten, too. It's there in the back of my head, but I can't quite pull it into the front of things, if you know what I mean."

"Same with me!" said Edward.

"Me too!" said Sophie.

"I know I'm forgetting something important," put in the pilot, frowning and tapping his forehead.

"I know!" said Hotspur, looking rather smug.

"Well, what is it, Mr Clever?" said Edward, a little crossly. After all, it is annoying when a little brother, who has just spoken for the first time, claims to remember something you have forgotten.

"Secret!" said Hotspur even more smugly.

Back, back, back they travelled, and somehow all things went wonderfully well. The snow was crisp. The sun kept its golden eye on them as they skiddoodled and skiddaddled and skiddeedled along, singing as they went. The pilot joined in cheerfully.

"We love the Antarctic," sang the new voice of Hotspur.

"A great place to be," agreed Edward quickly adding a line of his own.

"We found *The Riddle*!" sang Bonniface and Corona, inventing as one explorer and smiling secretly from skiddoo to skiddoo.

"We set the ghost free," Sophie finished the song for them, remembering that last radiant smile of mysterious Captain Cathcardo as she did so.

And for a while they fell silent, all thinking their own thoughts, while the silence of the Antarctic arched over them.

"There! There!" shouted Bonniface suddenly. And

sure enough, there ahead of them they could see the long green sheds of Scott Base. The pilot shouted with pleasure. He was longing for a cup of tea.

Bonniface and Corona looked deeply into each other's eyes across the snow that separated the blue and red skiddoos. They were both longing for a quick cup of tea, to be followed quickly by an Antarctic wedding, with a big party afterwards.

Edward found he was longing for sausages cooked on a barbecue. Hotspur wanted to dance in the snow, make a snowman and throw snowballs at his brother and sister.

Sophie wanted something too. She wanted to remember what it was she knew she was somehow forgetting... some special, happy thing that was dancing like a dream in the back of her mind.

They slid in between the green sheds, parked the skiddoos, sniffed the Scott Base air, and then sniffed again. The air smelt delicious. It smelt of roast turkey, onions, potatoes, green peas and steamed pudding. Bonniface shouted, and a whole lot of people (all wearing five layers of Antarctic clothes) came running to greet them, waving their mitts high in the air and cheering as they ran. In between cheers they were shouting something over and over again.

"Happy Christmas! Happy Christmas!" everyone was calling out to them.

"Oh! Of course!" cried Sophie. " Fancy forgetting Christmas!"

"There's been so much else to think about," said Edward. "And it seems as if everything has happened in just one day."

"Happy Christmas!" they shouted back, leaping off the skiddoos and dancing happily.

"It's wonderful to see you all safe and smiling," said one of the men. "We did check on that exploded helicopter you told us about, but it had blown itself into black dust. It must have been a tremendously efficient explosion."

"I had the strangest feeling while we were looking at that dust," said another man. "I glanced up and thought I saw three misty figures fighting with one another. But when I blinked and looked again they were gone."

"I saw them too," exclaimed a third man. "It was highly spooky. Personally, I think that the place where that helicopter crashed is going to be haunted from now on."

"But you are safe," cried one of the women. "Tell us all about your adventures. Tell us everything about everything."

How wonderful it was to be unexpected Antarctic discoverers with stories to tell, carols to sing and a delicious Christmas dinner waiting for them all!